Best Wishes,

Dennis [illegible]

2/15/98

. . . The Ravel'd Sleave of Care

. . . THE RAVEL'D SLEAVE OF CARE

Dennis K. Murphy

VANTAGE PRESS
New York / Washington / Atlanta
Los Angeles / Chicago

FIRST EDITION

Published by Vantage Press, Inc.
516 West 34th Street, New York, New York 10001

Manufactured in the United States of America
ISBN: 533-06225-X

Library of Congress Catalog Card No.: 84-90169

To the two women in my life: Brenda and Yvonne

Methought I heard a voice cry, "Sleep no more!
Macbeth does murder sleep!" the innocent sleep,
Sleep that knits up the ravel'd sleave of care,
The death of each day's life, sore labor's bath,
Balm of hurt minds, great nature's second course,
Chief nourisher in life's feast.

MACBETH, Act II, scene ii

. . . The Ravel'd Sleave of Care

CHAPTER ONE

Rollie sat staring at the water. It was a bright day in September, and he should not have been so gloomy. Yet he could not shake that feeling of depression; Anna hadn't meant that much to him, he thought, but that feeling persisted.

He remembered their first meeting and the wonderful time they had discussing his many literary heroes; he was pleased that Anna was so knowledgeable about them. He had been attracted to her, a young, beautiful American abroad, and he admitted to a brief affair—but that was over. In fact, it had been the realization of his betrayal of his own family that assured him of the senselessness of the affair and of his need to be with his wife and children.

As Rollie stared aimlessly over the almost motionless water before him, he could not help but think that only two weeks ago such a sight would have made him think only of Barbara and the children. He would have smiled with contentment at such thoughts. But today he did not have that feeling—and it bothered him a great deal.

Roland Christopher Welch, son of a hardworking steelworker who had emigrated from Dublin in 1919, had met Anna on his most recent trip to Ireland. Rollie had taken the family to visit the island for the first time during the summer of 1974. It was only for two weeks, but it had been an enjoyable trip. Aside from the fact that he had practically panicked at the thought of driving from Shannon to Limerick at night, on the left side of the road, and in a car that had the steering column on the right side, Rollie thoroughly enjoyed the countryside and Irish customs during those two weeks. The rest of the family did, too, yet no one but Rollie felt the urgency to return. Barbara, his wife, would like to have visited a warmer climate if that much money were to be spent again; the kids were ready for college and couldn't muster any enthusiasm for a revisit. So, in August 1976, Rollie decided to return by himself.

☆ ☆ ☆

Rollie was much more courageous on this visit; driving wasn't the challenge it had been two years before. After all, if Rollie could drive in New York City at rush hour, why would he get nervous at the prospect of driving from Shannon to Limerick, or even in Dublin, where the traffic was mild compared to that in New York City?

When he got to Dublin, the first stop on the trip (which made him wonder why he flew to Shannon rather than to Dublin), Rollie managed to find his way to the Hollyrood on Harcourt, just south of Saint Stephen's Green. The hotel was old, but spacious. The ceilings were about twelve feet high, and the large double bed was dwarfed in the huge room. Although there was no shower, he could at least be thankful for the private bath. Most of the hotels and B and B's had common baths where there was a fifty-pence charge for each bath. In the Hollyrood, the bath was free.

Parking always presented a problem in downtown Dublin; the streets were narrow and crowded, parking spaces and garages scarce. Fortunately, the Hollyrood had reserved two spaces in the alley behind the hotel for guest parking, and Rollie—the American—got one of those spaces. He discovered soon enough that the "reservation" meant only that as long as his car was in that space, it was reserved. Whether or not the space would be available should he vacate it for a while was pure speculation. However, it took Rollie less than half a day to decide upon public transportation. *No sense battling that traffic,* he thought, *especially since everything is accessible either by walking or the bus.* The car would be of more use when he left Dublin and headed for the country.

After he had unpacked a few things, Rollie went downstairs to the lobby. The clerk had asked him to leave the room key on the hook at the desk. *Not very secure,* Rollie thought, but the keys for all the hotel rooms were hanging there. He glanced to his left and saw the dining room. Nothing fancy, but there were linen cloths on the wooden tables and the glasses seemed clean. (He remembered the greasy glaze that coated the dishes and silver on his former visit, and he thought that maybe in the intervening two years some of the restaurants had invested in the American dishwasher!) Although he had not yet had his first Irish Tourist Board breakfast, he really looked forward to the rasher of bacon, white and brown bread, orange juice, scrambled eggs, and the ever-present box of Kelloggs cornflakes. "General Mills must make a fortune in Ireland alone," he audibly grunted, unaware of both the inaccuracy of his thought and the half-sleeping man in the parlor. Rollie got a strange, quizzical look, but nothing more.

It was pleasant outside; the sun was shining, and although it was a bit windy, the temperature was agreeable—of the light-sweater variety. Rollie stood on the steps of the hotel wondering why breakfast was so late. On his last trip, he recalled the landlord's insisting that breakfast be taken from seven-thirty to eight-thirty and here it was after eight and the dining room was still locked. Rollie could smell food cooking, so he knew it wouldn't be long, but the Irish ways continued to puzzle him.

"Would you be after having some breakfast?" a voice from the slightly ajar door asked. Rollie turned to see a young girl, with shocking red hair and freckles, covered in what he thought a hideous ankle-length, coarse dress.

"Thank you," he said. "I am hungry." Rollie made his way to the dining room and sat at a narrow table in the corner. The juice and cornflakes were already set out, so it was just a matter of telling the girl when to bring the scrambled eggs and bacon. (Rollie had tried the sausage once, but for some reason the Irish didn't cook it as thoroughly as the Americans. Rollie thought that it might have been the sausage that had made Jerry sick on the first trip.) The soda bread was plentiful; the meal was good. When he had downed his single cup of instant coffee—Rollie had forgotten how terrible the coffee was, that he really must order tea—he left the dining room satisfied. There was something about this breakfast: you knew what you would get tomorrow, and you looked forward to it. *I guess it's like the American who always orders the New York strip; you just never tire of it,* he thought.

Rollie planned to call Myra as soon as he arrived in Dublin. During the '74 visit, Myra had scolded him for having spent the better part of two weeks on the island before calling from the airport on the last day. *But you don't call anyone at nine o'clock in the morning on Saturday, even in Ireland,* he thought, and decided that a walk down to the green would be pleasant and would use an hour or two before he made the call. Myra certainly wouldn't be upset that he waited until she was up for the day!

Rollie wondered why so many people were already on the green. It was Saturday morning, so there weren't the usual number of office workers around, although the merchants appeared to be readying themselves for a very busy day. There must have been a lot of tourists. Perhaps it wasn't too early to call Myra.

Glancing to one side, Rollie spotted a tourist board office and immediately started for the door. Since no other customers appeared to be inside the office, he thought this an excellent time to make arrangements for his stay in Galway the following week. He tried the door, but it was locked. A little sign at eye level and just above the handle directed him to the office two blocks down the street, just across from the Mansion House. When Rollie turned the corner and caught sight of the long line, he knew that he had not been the first to approach the board office that morning. Disheartened, he cancelled his plans for that part of his morning activities.

Rollie was standing on Dawson Street and turned to face the imposing structure of the Royal Irish Academy Library. It was too early to get into the building—if, in fact, one could get into such a building, since so many of the Irish official places were impossible to visit—but just standing there looking at it, especially the way the sun seemed to glance off the shiny section of the outside staircase, was refreshing. Since the tourist board was out of the question, Rollie continued down Dawson to Nassau and took that crooked bend around the corner to the entrance to Trinity College. He walked through the archway to the interior, wondering if there would be a guard inside to ask for credentials. There was no guard, nor should there have been; all was peaceful around the lovely green quadrangle that graced the area separating the many buildings. Rollie couldn't help but remember the stories James had told about the old professor at Trinity who insisted on calling role when it was obvious that only one member of the class was present and of the professor who lectured to an empty class, each fifteen minutes or so pausing to ask the ghostly class if there were any questions!

Rollie left Trinity and continued down College Street to D'Olier and eventually O'Connell Street. He walked somewhat aimlessly, yet with a subconscious desire to see the Liffey. It was a joke in America, at least among Rollie's friends, that Guiness stout must have been so good because it was brewed from the water of the river Liffey, water so polluted that in '74 it seemed thick enough to walk across without getting wet! He now saw the Liffey again, and it hadn't changed: the green, murky water still made its way through the downtown section of Ireland's largest and busiest city. Rollie was preoccupied with the Liffey; he wondered if Dubliners ever noticed it at all.

These wanderings this morning took time, and when Rollie finally looked at his watch he was mildly shocked to discover that it was already noon. He decided to take a shortcut back to the Hollyrood and headed down Aston Quay to Parliament, got hopelessly lost, retraced his steps, and an hour later wound up at Wicklow and Grafton. It was easy enough from there, but what a waste of time. (Only Americans worried about wasted time.) It was two-thirty before he placed the call to Myra.

"Pack your things and stay with us. It's no trouble. We've planned to have you," Myra's excited voice spoke over the telephone.

Rollie hesitated, then answered, "I'm already booked for the day, and being at such a central point really makes it easier to get around. I won't have to keep asking you for directions."

"Nonsense," Myra answered. "I won't have you stay in that old, rundown hotel."

The argument went nowhere; the topic soon changed. Myra wanted to see Rollie as soon as possible, and so did James. During the '74 visit, James had just left on his holiday to Greece, and this time he wanted to be certain that he was at home to show Rollie a good time. James was Myra's only son, and since Martin had died, the tie between mother and son had grown stronger. James had intended to marry, but for the past year and a half he had put such plans out of mind, at least until he felt that Myra could get along by herself.

Rollie's father had been born in Dublin and stayed there until he was nineteen years old; he was the last of fifteen children to go to America. Desmond had loved his native land, and despite the fact that all his brothers and sisters had departed for the "American side," as they said, he felt certain that he and his dad would keep the butcher shop going forever. Two years later, Desmond was applying for a job in the Pittsburgh steel mills, just as his brother had done several years before.

Myra Connolly was Desmond's aunt, and although she knew the inevitable departure would take place, she sympathized with Desmond and truly had hoped that he could remain in Ireland. But such was not to be. Since she was the closest, if only, relative of Rollie, Myra decided that when Rollie appeared at her doorstep in August, she would be a better host than in '74. She would introduce Rollie "around," just to make his stay more pleasant.

"All right then, I'll expect to see you about seven. I'll be standing on the steps out in front." Rollie hung up and climbed the stairs to his room. There weren't any phones in the rooms, which was just as well. Rollie still didn't understand how to operate them. He followed the directions and would place two ten-pence pieces into the machine, but he was never successful (at least by himself) at making any voice connections. He wondered if all Americans had the same problem or if it was just a quirk with him. Whenever he had problems with the phone, he felt that people were watching him, and he often detected a wry smile whenever he asked for help!

Myra Connolly was about sixty years old and had as much pep as any thirty-five–year–old. She talked about all the Irish whiskey she and James would drink from time to time, but Rollie had doubts about the truth of that story. He never saw her drink more than an ounce or two in an evening. She always gave the excuse that since she was the one who was driving she really couldn't afford to get "tight." But Rollie suspected that she would make some other excuse if she were not the one driving.

Myra arrived promptly at seven to pick up Rollie, and within thirty minutes they were through the city and at Myra's place near Clentarf. James greeted them as the Volkswagon rolled into the drive, and from that point Rollie had one of the best times he could ever remember.

There were only a few guests, but all were delightful people. James introduced Rollie to his fiancée, Pat Hardy; Sean O'Donnell and his wife, Kitty, neighbors and good friends to both James and Myra; Jack O'Neil, a close friend of James who had taken classes with him at Trinity, and Anna Barton, Jack's steady.

Rollie found it difficult to keep from watching Anna; he thought she was beautiful. (Anna K. Barton was her full name, the K. standing for Karenina; her mother loved Tolstoy and would have named a son Leo, but she had a daughter!) Anna was slender, yet strong-looking. Rollie was overcome by her beautiful red hair, almost like that of the waitress at the Hollyrood that morning. (Anna's clothes, however, assured him that she wasn't a country girl.) It was easy to talk with her; her interests were varied and her knowledge of things American was evident. (Rollie later discovered that Anna was not Irish, but had come to Ireland on a visit several years before, shortly after she had finished college. She had planned to stay one year, but now, several years later, she had absolutely no desire to leave.)

Rollie monopolized Anna, but no one seemed to mind. Everyone was having a good time singing, drinking, telling stories, and eating. Rollie wanted to know at length what Anna found so attractive about Ireland, why she had decided to stay, and what her plans were. The more he drank, the less cogent his arguments became in his efforts to convince her that she should return to America.

About ten-thirty, Myra announced that a second serving of

bacon and eggs was ready. With all that drinking, Rollie was happy to eat again. He had no difficulty polishing off two eggs, four crisp pieces of bacon (not those chunks like this morning!), several slices of toasted soda bread, and a "few" more ounces of Paddy.

Anna was marvelous. She seemed to drink just as much as Rollie, and he was convinced that she didn't at all mind making him feel welcome. The next day, Rollie would wonder what Jack had been thinking about all of this time, but for the present such thoughts never entered his mind. Anna was so warm, her voice so pleasing. And often she would lean over to Rollie and gently lay her head on his shoulder. It seemed so natural and good to Rollie.

It was about twelve-thirty when James drove Rollie back to the Hollyrood. James was alert, and his conversation revealed that he had not drunk nearly so much as Rollie. Rollie had not intended to drink more than one or two glasses, especially on this first night in Dublin, but the party, friends, and atmosphere had made it too easy. He was worried, though, that he would be troubled with a hangover on the morning of his second day! Myra had assured him that as long as he kept to the Paddy and nothing else, he would feel fine come morning. Rollie earnestly hoped that Myra was right!

James reminded Rollie that plans were made to attend the Abbey the next night, and as Rollie left the car he could remember only vaguely having made such plans. Rollie tried to enter the Hollyrood, but the door was locked. Fortunately, one of the night men happened to be at the desk, and he opened the door for Rollie. Rollie had forgotten about ringing the bell after midnight and wondered how long he would have stood at the door waiting before realizing what to do. As he passed the desk, Rollie took his room key from the hook, climbed the stairs to his room, unlocked it quietly, opened and closed the door a little less quietly, quickly undressed, and fell into bed. He was surprised that his head wasn't swirling, as it so often had during his college days after such drinking. He fell asleep wondering what had happened to Anna and where she had gone. What a wonderful two weeks this was going to be!

CHAPTER TWO

Rollie lay in bed for a long time, thinking about the night before. Myra had tried to convince him to abandon the Hollyrood and take the room available at her house. She was very persuasive, insisting that Martin's room was never used and that a guest for a week or two certainly wouldn't upset anything at all in the household.

He thought, too, of Anna and the long conversation they had had. Rollie fancied himself an authority on Orwell ever since he discovered that the author had written works other than *1984* and *Animal Farm*. It was during the '74 trip that he discovered *Down and Out in Paris and London*, and from that time on his appetite for Orwell only grew stronger. He could talk for hours about all the characters and loved to compare plots to try to discover elements of similiarity that would reveal to the astute reader little things so characteristic of Orwell. He remembered that Anna had talked with some assuredness about Orwell; she, too, had read some of his early novels and enjoyed them a great deal. Rollie particularly enjoyed Orwell's description of the horrible sequence of events in the underground kitchens of Paris, the long hours of work in the greasy and smoky rooms, and the very short days of sleep for the tired workers. It appalled him to think that anyone could leave a fourteen-hour kitchen shift, walk home, and drop into bed, still clothed in the same stinking rags that had been worn at work. He could smell it, and he could see the roaches crawling on the corners of the unmade bed. Anna had talked knowledgeably about these things, too, but she didn't like to dwell upon them so much as Rollie did.

Rollie also thought about home. He had wanted Barbara to come with him; he thought it would have been nice for just the two of them to vacation for a couple of weeks. The children had always been part of past vacations, and as pleasant as it had been to have them along, there is something to say for the privacy of a married couple without children for a few days. But Barbara had remained adamant on this issue. Yes, she did want a vacation without the children, but not in Ireland. "Let's try a new place, perhaps somewhere in the United States. Why not Florida? We've never been there," she said. Barbara had left for her mother's house in Decorah, Iowa, two days before Rollie flew to Shannon.

His head felt clear, so Rollie tried standing. Myra had assured him there would be no hangover with Paddy, and so far she was right. He moved across the room to the bath, looking forward to a warm shower, which he had forgotten was not part of these accommodations. He settled for a hot bath, and it really wasn't so bad. He shaved and dressed and then glanced at his watch. It was still early and he was hungry, yet he had missed the hotel breakfast. He knew there was a McDonald's a few blocks down on Grafton, and he hoped that the Irish had also adopted the American McDonald custom of adding breakfast to the regular hamburger fare. It still amazed him how quickly American ideas spread to Europe and how easy it was to travel abroad and find so many adaptations of the stateside fast-food business. Perhaps that was one of the reasons Barbara couldn't get excited about another trip to Ireland; she often said that it was silly to travel thousands of miles to get something one could find within a block of home.

It was raining this morning and much colder than the day before. Rollie had to return to his room for a jacket and hat and then proceed to McDonald's. He never thought of calling to check on the opening time of the restaurant, and he was surprised (and wet) when he found the door to the restaurant locked.

"Hello! We've been trying to get you for the last two hours," the voice said excitedly from the other end. It was James and he wanted to invite Rollie to join them for dinner before the theater.

"I got so damn mad when I couldn't find any place open for breakfast," Rollie answered, "that I went back to bed." The wet, cold, and hunger took its toll, and the maid couldn't arouse Rollie when James had first called. The sleep had done some good, and although his first attempt at facing the awakened world that morning found him feeling only slight effects from the night before, now he was completely refreshed.

"Sure. That would be fine with me. I'll meet you at Snaffles about six," and Rollie hung up the phone.

What started out as a bad day was beginning to hold promise of being a not-so-bad day! Rollie couldn't help but think about Anna as he tried the tub for a second time that day. He pictured her a beautiful colleen, yet he knew very well that Barton was no more Irish than Smith. He mused that she must have thought him a terrible bore, yet his memory indicated that she had had just as fine a time as he. Rollie wondered if this evening would again provide the opportunity for as much conversation as the night before; he wondered, too, whether or not Jack would be so magnanimous as on Saturday. Rollie ventured to guess that the only time Jack got to talk to Anna that night was on the way to the party and on the way home. Even the hour in the garden behind Myra's house was an uninterrupted time when Rollie and Anna were completely alone. She had become engrossed in Rollie's stories about his '74 trip, the bathing in Galway Bay, the soccer game at Clonbur, and even Jerry's ill-timed sickness for the entire three days at Salthill. On occasion that evening, Anna had pressed her body close to his, as if understanding became easier when they were touching. It was thoughts such as these that occupied Rollie as he shaved and caused him—perhaps–to fail to notice the water flowing over the sides of the sink. No damage was done, and a quick wipe with the bath towel took care of matters. Rollie was anticipating another enjoyable evening with friends.

James and Myra were there, overtly cheerful and ready as ever to start partying once again. Rollie was not surprised to see Pat, and he was very happy to see Anna, but he wondered where Jack was. Anna explained that Jack had an early-morning sales obligation in Cork and had decided to take the afternoon train so that he could be fresh the next morning. It was a new account, and, difficult as it was to promote a new line of footwear, Jack had decided that this time he should give it his best. Through the conversation on Saturday, Rollie had learned that Jack, after he had received his diploma from Trinity, had decided not to pursue law—he really had some strong doubts about his ability to master the law examinations—and welcomed the opportunity to become the sole representative of Florsheim Shoes in Ireland. For the past two years, he had had difficulty meeting his sales obligations, but in the past several months business had taken a turn for the better. He didn't know whether it was the Irish or tourists who were beginning to take to the Florsheim line, but he really didn't care. His American training course, which had been paid for by the company and had given Jack his first opportunity to visit New York City, now was beginning to have results; at least, that is what he believed. The Cork account could mean a very sizable market, so, party or not, he would not miss this opportunity to establish himself in that area.

Snaffles had a limited menu, but the entrées were excellent. Rollie decided upon veal oscar, by no means an exclusively European dish, but certainly a cosmopolitan one. *In these days of rocketing prices,* he thought, *six pounds fifty isn't so expensive.* And, as was so often the case in Ireland, the tip was included. The wine was good, too. A moderately priced French Bordeaux was chosen in order to accent the beef plates of the others, but Rollie thought it went well enough with the veal.

Anna sat beside Rollie. It was so easy to talk with her; it seemed they had been friends for years. She wore a lovely wool dress of rich brown and green tweed, or so Rollie thought. He couldn't tell you what the current fashions were, but he knew when someone looked sharp. He had only seen Anna in two outfits, yet he imagined that anything she wore would compliment her beautiful red hair. This evening, she wore her hair down, and it fell to just below her shoulders. It was full and smooth, and even in the dimmed lights of the restaurant, it glistened. For Rollie, Anna seemed to radiate beauty.

When they had entered the dining room at Snaffles, Myra had insisted that Rollie sit between her and Anna so that he could be shared equally. At first, Rollie talked almost exclusively to Anna, but as time passed he reminded himself that Myra and James felt most responsible to help him have a pleasant, if not exciting, time in Dublin. So he endeavored to include all of them in the conversation. He was clumsy in this maneuver, however, for when he turned to face James and Myra, he involuntarily excluded Anna. This dinner did not run as smoothly as he had hoped.

The play was to start at eight o'clock, and since there might be some difficulty with parking, James suggested that they leave by seven-thirty at the latest. He had already purchased the tickets, so that matter was taken care of, but traffic on Sunday evening was always surprisingly heavy. And although the Abbey wasn't that far from Snaffles, one must drive down Grafton, and that could cause some delay.

They left promptly at seven-thirty and arrived at the Abbey about ten minutes to eight. It was Rollie's first time there, and he was surprised at the comfort and intimacy of the little theatre. Both James and Pat had seen the play previously, but had liked it well enough to try again. Myra and Rollie had not seen it before, and Anna would not be attending. As it turned out, it was just coincidence that Anna had been at dinner. Originally she was to have accompanied Jack to Cork, but something had come up at work and she was obligated to attend to the matter. She had called James that afternoon to alter some plans that Jack had made for the four of them for Wednesday, and it was then that James had invited her to join them for dinner. Rollie should have realized that neither James nor Myra would deliberately have tried to "fix him up" with anyone. They both knew Barbara and the children, and in '74 they had enjoyed the meeting, however short it had been. But Rollie was noticeably annoyed that Anna would not be with them for the remainder of the evening.

The play did not go well. The comedy did not affect Rollie in the least. Nothing was funny; it was just boring. *It was cruel,* he thought, *for Anna to have acted so friendly, to lead me on with all those smiles and touches. He felt as though she had betrayed him. Could he have imagined what had happened on Saturday? Surely, Anna had been interested in him and in what he had to say. Yes, he was married, and happily so, but this was different.* Rollie couldn't understand how she could so casually have told him about her planning to stay with Jack those few days in Cork. Didn't she know how much she had become "Rollie's girl" on this best of all vacations?

The bar opened at intermission, and James raced to get some Paddy for the group. But the glow that Rollie had felt earlier was gone, and Paddy didn't seem to matter. He took it, but he didn't care about it. He could feel the urge to drink for another reason, that reason he so often resorted to back at the lake. It was something to do; it was a way of getting rid of the day and work, a way to prepare for sleep. Often Rollie's few nighttime drinks got him to sleep quickly, but awakened him early as well—about 2:30 A.M.—and he never could get back to sleep.

This night, he resisted and called it quits after just that one drink. When the play had ended, he thanked Myra and James for the evening and promised to call them before he left Dublin and Ireland. No, he had decided to forego their offer this time, but perhaps another occasion would present itself when he might stay at their home. He thought he would turn in the car on Monday and take the train to Athlone; he had always wanted to go fishing on the river Shannon, and this was as good a time as any. He would be through Dublin again before returning to America. He did have plans to visit London and Paris, just for a few days, and he wanted to take the boat from Dublin to Holyhead.

The parting was not nearly so warm and cordial as the night before. Rollie knew his feelings were transparent, but he didn't care. He wanted to get Anna out of his mind, and the best way to do that would be to leave Dublin and these people. Rollie was a moody person; he could be caustic, at times, even to his friends. Tonight he stopped short of being caustic, but he certainly was not at all engaging. After all, he was over forty, and sulking when you don't get your way was so like an adolescent. He knew all of this, yet he was convinced that he would never rid himself of these vestiges of earlier years.

☆ ☆ ☆

The train stopped abruptly at the station. There were no signs to indicate where they were; there was no conductor to announce the stop. Rollie thought he had seen a sign on one of the buildings as the train crossed the bridge, but he wasn't sure. He knew there was no Athlone Hotel, and he didn't see any billboard, as he most likely would have seen in America. It seemed to him that such practice was an Irish guessing game: where am I? Sometimes you win; other times you lose. As he continued to struggle with the indifference of the evening before, he lifted his two bags to the station platform. The train pulled out almost immediately, and he was left standing, alone, wondering where he was.

His initial attempt to leave the platform was thwarted by a locked door. He could see people sitting on benches inside, but he couldn't figure out how to get to them. He tried another door, and that, too, was locked. Rollie began to get angry. He spotted a staircase and carried his bags down to the lower level. The waiting room was unassuming, and so were the people. No one appeared to notice him, and that irritated him almost as much as the locked doors. He wanted someone to ask if he needed assistance; it was obvious that he was becoming a very perplexed man! He did not see the clerk behind the glass window as he struggled through the swinging doors into the street.

Across from the station stood a stone wall about fifteen feet high, which stretched in either direction as far as he could see. He learned later that the Athlone army barracks were there, but at this time he grew more angry at not knowing his whereabouts.

Just as he was about to leave his bags and seek help within the station, an old man came through the doors and asked if he needed a taxi. Rollie certainly did need one, if only to discover where he was.

"A pound twenty downtown," the man said and made no effort either to get Rollie's bags or to indicate where the cab was.

"Where are we?" Rollie asked, and his tone betrayed just a bit of that annoyance that surely Myra and James could not have missed the night before.

"In the city," he said. "Do you have a room?" At this point, it was obvious that the man did not realize that Rollie couldn't be certain that this city was Athlone.

"Is this Athlone?" Rollie asked.

"Aye, it is." A simple and direct answer.

"Would you take me to Mrs. Malone's on Roundtree?"

"Just put your bags here," the man said, and Rollie hoisted them into the small trunk. *Just like New York,* he thought as he climbed into the front seat—on the left! At least, he remembered that much.

It was just a bit after noon when Mrs. Malone welcomed Rollie to the house. Roundtree was only about 700 yards from the station, and although it was a very walkable distance, it wasn't so easy with two heavy bags. Rollie could have kicked himself for traveling so heavy when it wasn't necessary. He never wore half the things he brought with him, whether on a long or short trip. (In '74 he had taken the train from Galway to Dublin and the bus from the Dublin station to the city center, assured by the conductor that Saint Stephen's Green was not at all distant from the point of departure. He remembered very clearly how he had struggled with those bags all the way from D'Olier up Grafton to Saint Stephen's Green North and to the Shelbourne Hotel, at each step cursing those extra clothes. The weather was so bad on that trip that he wore the same warm clothes for six days in a row!) He could have walked today, but he did not want aching arms on what was to be "his" vacation.

Mrs. Malone's was a fairly modern home, and there was a bath and shower for the guest rooms. Three people shared the bathroom, but it was clean and attractive, freshly painted with a soft rose flat on the upper walls and an off-white gloss on the bottom sections. There was heat, too, a commodity often scarce in the B and B's. (One house in Limerick charged fifty pence per night for heat.) So often the lady of the house would offer the missus additional blankets and a hot-water bottle for night comfort, so the heat in Mrs. Malone's seemed rather extravagant, but Rollie did not complain. The daily price for lodging was a reasonable nine pounds—twice what it had been in '74—but well within the current range of prices. Rollie's room was to the left as you entered the front door, with a view of the front yard. Mrs. Malone was a meticulous gardener, and the variety of flowers that wound between the luscious green sections of lawn attested to that fact.

"If you'd care for high tea," Mrs. Malone said, "I'd like to know now. My husband will be home around five, and I want to make preparations. I expect some Germans in this afternoon, too, and they might want to eat." Rollie thanked her, but declined the offer. Jerry, a friend from home, had visited Athlone two years before and had told Rollie about the Prince of Wales Hotel, with cuisine fit for a king! Rollie decided that tonight would be a good time to discover the truth in that recommendation.

Rollie stayed at Mrs. Malone's only long enough to place some things in the bureau drawer; he wanted to get downtown and look around. It was windy and chilly, but since the sun was shining, Rollie thought it a good day for a walk. It took about fifteen minutes to reach the main street through town and Rollie's almost reflex action directed him immediately to the tourist board office. (For Rollie, Bord Failte had become synonymous with travel in Ireland.) The first thing he asked about was fishing, and the very congenial lady in the office directed him to Mr. McDougal's home, just five minutes down the road. There wasn't much else Rollie had envisioned doing in Athlone, since, as far as he could see, the town didn't even have a movie theater. Rollie wasted no time inquiring at Mr. McDougal's, where he was told, by a woman whom he presumed was Mrs. McDougal, that the mister would not return until tomorrow morning and that nine o'clock would be the best time to catch him. Rollie would be there at nine.

Around six o'clock, Rollie decided to head for the Prince of Wales, so he asked Mrs. Malone if he might use her telephone to call a taxi. Rollie had returned to his room near five-thirty, after having taken the tour of downtown. There wasn't much to see, but he did wander down to the docks to check on the boats, thirty- and forty-footers, apparently owned by local people. *There must have been wealth somewhere nearby to afford* those *boats,* he thought. He fancied himself hiring one for tomorrow's fishing and wondered if any belonged to Mr.

McDougal. Perhaps this trip would turn out all right.

"Mr. James is out tonight. Sorry," came the reply. Rollie had called every taxi listed in the book, but none was available. One even explained that he never went out at night with his car, especially in the rain. Rollie was not at all pleased with these calls, and he felt helpless. Mr. Malone, home from his trip to Ballyclare, insisted that he take Rollie to the Prince of Wales. Rollie thanked him and took the ride, but couldn't help but think that Mrs. Malone probably had a great deal to do with the arrangements. The "Germans" were in, and she seemed pleased with that fact.

"Welch, you cluck!" Rollie muttered. The menu did suggest a martini before dinner, but by this time Rollie should have remembered there was no gin in the Irish martini, just dry vermouth. The fifty-pence drink just sat there untouched.

The dining room was attractive, the service satisfactory. It was nothing like the Green Isle Motel, he thought, yet pretty good for such an out-of-the-way place. But you still got the feeling that the Irish cared little for the vacuum cleaner: the rugs appeared greasy and soiled from both food and wear. Rollie had distinctly remembered that Irish restaurants, especially in the smaller towns, were not bent upon cleanliness, the Beehive Cafe in Ennis being his most often quoted referent. But that thought aside, the meal tonight was excellent, although expensive, and after he had finished he headed straight for the bar. A little lager would hit the spot.

Anna crept back into his thoughts, but the morrow's fishing on the Shannon kept him from another night of self-pity and brooding. He did wonder what she was doing this night, if Jack had returned early, and if she was visiting the Connolly's or out on her own. It never occurred to Rollie that the past weekend was as much a treat and unusual turn of events for her as it was for him. Vacations seem to do that to people: they often forget that how they live while on vacation is not how they live at other times and that those whom they visit are not on vacation! And then Rollie wondered why anyone would choose to live forty or more weeks each year as each of us does.

One lager led to another; Rollie soon forgot about Anna and the rain. He began to concentrate on the three girls who had come into the bar shortly after he. They had ordered a drink—Rollie didn't know what—which the bartender mixed with what appeared to beer and a lemon syrup. By the time he noticed the bartender mixing the drink, he was a few too many lagers along to discern the ingredients. A happy glow came over him; he had a notion to talk to the girls, yet he was just as content to sit there at the bar and imagine what they were talking about or what they might do had he approached them. He had now been in Ireland three days, and the lake at home seemed so much a part of some other life. Teaching was fine, but the freedom to travel at leisure seemed his due and so much more meaningful than his daily battles with homework and unruly children.

Rollie was anything but a night owl; often he went to bed very early, especially when he had had a martini or two before five o'clock. But tonight he surprised himself by sitting there at the bar until closing at eleven-thirty. He wasn't concerned at all about his earlier evening, getting a taxi, or the rain. Drink did that to him. He felt that he could walk fairly steady as he left the hotel bar, and he hazarded an inward guess that Mrs. Malone's was about ten minutes down the road. The rain had stopped, and as he left the Prince of Wales, he turned right and headed toward Mrs. Malone's, which *was* about ten minutes down the road. He felt good about that, and once in his warm bed he could only think about the morning and fishing on the Shannon. He dreamed about the boats and a large catch, never once considering what he would do with a large catch.

CHAPTER THREE

Barbara stepped onto the porch and asked Rollie if he'd like a cup of coffee. He accepted, but it didn't shake him from the depression he felt this morning, and every morning for that matter, since he had returned from his trip to Ireland. Barbara had been in Decorah part of that time and had enjoyed the visit. She had spent several days with her mother and a few with her sister Polly. Polly and Mike had married shortly after Barbara and Rollie, and it was always fun to visit them. Mike was a building engineer at the Crane Company, and, as far as Barbara knew, did pretty well. Polly always seemed to have the best clothes, and the three children rarely wanted for anything. Barbara and Rollie often remarked that they would never have raised their children like that; it would spoil them. Yet Chris, Joan, and Bruce never gave the appearance of spoiled children, and Rollie and Barbara had spent quite a few weeks at Polly and Mike's place over the years. Perhaps it was a usually suppressed feeling that Barbara and Rollie had about their own children that manifested itself in their remarks about her sister's children.

Barbara could sew, and sew she did. She made all of her own clothes, except for those hand-me-downs from her mother and the few gifts that came now and then. The family was always well dressed, and at little physical or emotional cost. They were a happy family.

Barbara did not recognize the gloom in Rollie this morning, for she was thinking about the good times she had spent in the Midwest these past two weeks while Rollie had been in Ireland.

* * *

Barbara was a dreamer, just like Rollie. So, when the opportunity arose during her stay at her mother's to go hiking, she had jumped at the chance. As a teenager, Barbara had loved to hike around the park and in the small mountainlike areas of Decorah. Iowa generally is fairly flat, so it was a bonus to have these kinds of hills so nearby. (Perhaps it was a geographical spillover from Minnesota!) Today, Barbara would relive those past years.

As she neared the top of Buck Trail, Barbara realized that she was completely alone for the first time since her visit had started three days before. There was no mother, father, sister, or friends to interfere; she had an afternoon to herself. Even the children, grown though they were, did not tag along. They had taken this opportunity to visit their former schoolmates from Decorah. It was not as though Barbara disliked her friends and relatives; after all, it was she who decided to visit them. But she had not been alone much, even during the past year, so this afternoon would give her time to think—more than she had had in a long, long time.

Barbara first thought about her marriage to Rollie and the difficulties they had had during those first years. She allowed herself to believe that Rollie became angry with her on the day they were married. He had denied it, of course, but Barbara felt differently. She had observed that Rollie had been uncharacteristically abrupt with her parents that day and seemed very displeased with her friends. Despite the fact that on many occasions Rollie professed how much he enjoyed the family gatherings, Barbara convinced herself that the truth of his feelings emerged on their wedding day, and she could never dismiss that thought, no matter how often Rollie tried to change her mind.

Barbara knew that Rollie loved her, and she never doubted his devotion and faithfulness to her. But she often thought that he would have been much happier with someone else—and perhaps she, too, may have been better off with another. The courtship lasted a full two years, so there was nothing rushed about the affair. But this uneasiness in her lingered, and the years only seemed to intensify it.

Barbara moved from the rock on which she was sitting to a log that overlooked the center of town. She could easily see the creek that ran behind the school and the new housing development that was rapidly growing on the south side of the city. Now she wondered how the development could ever be filled, since the population of Decorah seldom changed and when it did, it grew smaller. Her brother Skip had built one of these new houses on the bluff, and she wondered how such a young man could afford to build a new house while he still owned a sizeable older one in town. Skip worked as night stock manager at the local Super Duper, and she thought that such a position certainly didn't give him the kind of money needed to keep up two households. Skip was engaged, but he had no intention of marrying in the near future. *Perhaps his expenses as a single man aren't that great,* she thought. Barbara had remained quite ignorant about the costs of living.

Her thoughts now shifted back to Rollie and their marriage. Aliceanne was born within the first anniversary of their marriage, and this pleased both Rollie and Barbara. They had both talked about having ten children and how good that would be for a marriage. She remembered how they had both talked about being drawn closer together through children and how Rollie seemed to be so concerned about her during her pregnancy. And when Aliceanne was born, Rollie did all that he could to make it comfortable for Barbara. He tried to do so much that often he got in the way. Barbara laughed to herself as she remembered the time he had had changing diapers, when his blunders caused her more work than if he had not even tried to help! But he did indeed make her feel special, and the marriage grew stronger.

Rollie had time for his friends, too, and when he brought someone home unannounced (as he often did), Barbara was there to fix sandwiches and lunch. But that, too, was part of their happiness, and she enjoyed helping him as much as he enjoyed helping her with Aliceanne. Barbara loved taking care of Aliceanne and Rollie. She did not feel deprived, nor did she feel the need to pursue a career. When the children were grown would be time enough to do other things; for now, she wanted only to raise a family and be happy with Rollie. He seemed to want the same.

Barbara thought about many of her friends who, over the past twenty years, had not been so fortunate as she. She remembered a close school friend, Betti Rosbann, whose marriage had been a great trial. Betti's husband, Porter, had never been able to accept marriage, espcecially when he and Betti had a child. Porter had behaved as though he were single, and he thought nothing of staying out without Betti on Saturday nights until all the bars had closed. Quite often he would be with his single friends, characteristically chasing after the village teenagers who had just graduated from high school. Betti had stood up well for a while, but the limit of her toleration came when Porter was arrested one night with several of his buddies and charged with molesting a minor. Betti never discovered whether or not Porter was actually a part of the affair or just a bystander. Nevertheless, she could tolerate him no longer. The marriage ended in divorce just seven months after their second child was born.

Barbara and Rollie had problems, but never anything more than little frustrations about money. Rollie, unlike so many of Barbara's friends' husbands, was most considerate and thoughtful of the family needs. Barbara remembered the weeks that the two of them spent home while their friends were dining out. They would liked to have done more partying, but they were more concerned to be with one another, and that made them happy—despite the lack of dinners out and parties.

Although Barbara did not have much opportunity to be with those school friends, who were so far away, she did make friends with the many neighbors who lived in the area. It was nice, too, that most of the neighbors had problems similar to those of Rollie and Barbara, so that daily conversations between the women as they took care of the children centered on topics of interest to them all. Although life was difficult for most of them in the neighborhood, Barbara knew it was easier for her because she had that support from Rollie. Times were difficult, but wasn't that so true for so many, and how many families could get through all of this with the love and concern that Barbara and Rollie shared? These were pleasant memories.

Barbara's thoughts were suddenly interrupted as she noticed

a movement in the bushes to her left; she did not sense any danger, but the movement did startle her momentarily. As she focused upon the spot from which she had heard movement, she spotted a raccoon. It was pretty to watch, but she knew the danger involved if she got too close to the animal. As she made a sudden movement to stand to get a better view, the raccoon disappeared in the underbrush. This diversion made her realize that she had been sitting on the log for quite a while and that her seat was damp. She brushed herself off and started down the side of the hill toward her mother's house. It was good to get away on these all too rare hikes; it always proved to be such positive therapy. These few minutes with her thoughts would serve to reaffirm her belief in the security of her life with Rollie.

When Barbara finally got back to the house, a few of her dad's friends were gathered in the garage to look at his latest acquisition, a 1939 Ford Tudor. It was remarkably well preserved and appeared as though it had seen little winter weather through the years. She later discovered that the car did indeed see little bad weather, but it had rusted out just the same, and a friend of her dad had restored it by replacing two of the fenders and the trunk cover. She greeted her dad and those friends whom she recognized and hurried into the house. By now it was very near dinnertime, and she knew that her mother, despite the fact that Barbara was a guest, expected her to help prepare supper. Preparation time had passed, so she rifled through the closet, found the whiskey and vermouth, and made a drink for her mother and herself. When all else fails, make a drink! Her mother never drank often, but she did like the festive Manhattans. (Rollie became an instant favorite when he introduced Helen to her first Manhattan, and each visit since, Helen acted as though it was her right to have those drinks.) Mixing the drinks was the easy way out; at least no explanations were needed for Barbara's late arrival—on her vacation.

Dinner that night was enjoyable. Polly and Mike were there; the children were not. For the first time in many years, the five adults dined without the ever-present din of children, grandchildren, and other relatives.

Polly talked about the children and told Barbara how wonderfully behaved Aliceanne and the boys were; Mike had been impressed with Jerry's artistic ability. Barbara's father talked about the time they all dined at the Sky Line, when Rollie had played the piano for them and they had had such a good time when her mother had had a little too much to drink and had uncharacteristically insisted upon dancing with all the young men on the floor. It went so well that after dinner, George suggested they go to the country club for an after-dinner drink, probably in the hopes that they might once again have an enjoyable night out. He acknowleged that Rollie was not there, but he knew that both Polly and Barbara were pretty good at the piano.

Once at the club, Barbara unexpectedly met a number of former high-school classmates, and she reminisced about the days that she had long ago decided were no longer worth thinking about. The drink undoubtedly aided her, but she seemed to revel in the company of these friends as she recounted the dances, the skating parties, and the class trip to Chicago. Barbara was never at a loss for words; she knew everyone and they remembered her. It all seemed like yesterday, so real and exciting.

Clark Axtell, the trumpet player in her high-school marching band and a person whom she wished she had dated more often, asked her to dance. Barbara remembered he had been a good dancer and now was pleased to find that he had not lost that talent. While they were dancing, he told her about his wife and children, mentioning the fact that she had died after the birth of their fourth child and that he had been raising the children by himself for the past ten years. She learned, too, of other friends who had been married and divorced; she learned of happy marriages. She felt sorry for many of the people he mentioned, but did not let those stories spoil her evening.

The night was filled with activity and ended just about at the right time. It was nearing midnight when Polly and Mike said good night and left for home. George and Helen had left earlier, so Barbara needed a ride. Clark offered, and Barbara accepted. The drive to her parent's home was short, so they had little time to talk at length. He left her at the doorstep and thanked her for the good time that evening. He said he hoped he might see her again before she returned to the lake. Barbara said good night and went into the house. By this time, George and Helen were asleep, but Barbara's mother had left the kitchen light on so that Barbara could find her way up the stairs without tripping over the boxes piled on the landing. She felt exhausted, but exhilarated. It had been a fun evening, and that's the way vacations should be.

She went into the bathroom and brushed her teeth. She glanced into the mirror and saw a vibrant and beautiful woman. She felt as good as she looked, and she attributed the feeling to those wonderful years of a happy marriage. She went to sleep secure in the thought that the routine of marriage had been good to her and that she and Rollie could not be happier.

CHAPTER FOUR

On Thursday, Barbara moved to Polly and Mike's for the remainder of her visit. Her mother and father had made plans in June to go to Chicago with Paul and Angie, two longtime neighbors and good friends, to attend the annual antiques exhibit, now being held in Mitchell Exhibition Center. Since Barbara's visit home was done on the spur of the moment, the move to Polly's went quite smoothly. In the past, the visits were always with Rollie, so the good times they had to talk about now had been built around what the four of them had done and the places they had been. But Barbara guessed that three of them could do just as well, at least with respect to dining out, visiting sights, and talking into the wee hours. (Often it was only Barbara, Polly, and Mike who talked through the night, since Rollie had great difficulty staying awake past eleven on any night.) Although Polly's children were a bit younger than Barbara's, they seemed to get along well together and all of them were happy enough to find their own sources of entertainment.

This night was an especially good one to be at Polly's because it was Mike's turn to host the Fish Tale Club, and those evenings always involved a lot of eating, drinking, singing, and story telling. Mike's friends would bring their wives, and all of them would have a real bash. They did this about twice a year, so Barbara was fortunate to have picked the right week. Mike's friends all knew Barbara, because Rollie and Barbara had, on several occasions in past years, been lucky enough to have visited Decorah at the time when the club had met.

The fish tales grew out of the stories that were told after the group's first opening day fishing campout in 1970. Iowa is not renowned for its trout fishing, and Decorah was fairly representative of the whole state in this regard. If it hadn't been for the few streams that flowed from the neighboring state of Minnesota, I suspect that the group would still be looking for its first catch. But they persisted, and as luck would have it, often they did catch enough to keep them in a meal or two on each outing. Mike felt that the true sportsman should bring only enough food on the trip to get him started that first day; thereafter, all entrées should be comprised of the day's catch.

The Fish Talers always left for camp on Friday afternoon, since the season traditionally opened at 10:00 A.M. on the following Saturday. If Mike were completely truthful with himself, he would have to admit that the Friday night meal was by far the best of the weekend, regardless of the size of the catch. Mike's duties for Friday were to supply the beer and munchies; he always brought two cases of Iowa's best. Rollie, a sometimes member of the fishing party if he happened to be in Iowa at the opportune moment, was assigned the task of providing "something extra," which usually meant a quart of Beefeaters and a very small bottle of vermouth. Karl always brought the dishes and utensils and shared the cost of the refreshments with Mike. But best of all was Hobie's contributions. Hobie never could get to camp as early as the others—he had more difficulty getting his work done early enough on Friday—but he had a penchant for doing what he did best on these trips: providing the steak, potatoes, and salad. It was always dark by the time Hobie arrived, and the others had already pitched the tent, scouted the stream for the best spots, and finished the last of the martinis. The steaks were always one-pound sirloins, the potatoes were Tater Tots (imagine trying to cook Tater Tots outside in thirty-degree weather), and the salad consisted of lovely large chunks of iceberg lettuce with Hobie's green goddess dressing. How Mike hated that green goddess.

By midnight, there was enough warmth in the tent to last at least until 3:00 or 4:00 A.M., and since they would get up soon after that in order to breakfast early and take places along the stream to await the 10:00 A.M. opening, they only froze for a few hours. The Saturday-morning breakfast was almost as welcome as the dinner the night before, with fried potatoes, eggs, sausage, bacon, soggy toast, and coffee or beer, whichever one was tempted to drink on that cold morning. Anticipation of a catch showed in the optimism of their talk; the eventual take, however, rarely equalled their expectations. But despite the fishing disappointments, not one of them would ever dream of being anywhere else on opening day.

Only once had any member of the group caught his limit within the first hour, and Mike was the lucky one. Barbara remembered Rollie telling about one morning, sitting about half a mile from Mike's spot, when he thought about giving up after only an hour of trying. He had nary a nibble in all that time, and yet this spot, when he scouted it on Friday afternoon, was filled with those beautiful one- and two-pounders. They were as wily as deer, he thought, which were so easy to spot out of season, yet able to stay almost invisible during the week of hunting season. At about the time Rollie was thinking of moving to another spot, Mike came walking up and asked how things were going.

"Any luck?" Mike asked.

"Terrible," came Rollie's reply. Hobie was just out of hearing range, but he could see the two talking. " I haven't got a fish even to smell the worm," he said disgustedly. "You blanked, too?"

"No, a little better than that," Mike answered.

"How many?" Rollie wanted to know.

"The limit." Mike smiled.

"Are you kidding me?" Rollie asked.

"They're not all two-pounders, but there is enough for a couple of meals for all of us," Mike continued.

"Where the hell were you, at that hole by the tree stump?" Rollie asked. He was certain that with all those anglers crowded around that spot no one would get much of anything, especially since they were making enough noise to scare away the bravest of fish.

"That's the place," Mike replied. "There must have been a lot of hungry ones in there, because they were really pulling them out," he said.

"Do you think I should go back and try it?" Rollie asked.

"Why not? Nobody can keep you out of there, and I don't see anyone else catching anything anywhere else," Mike said.

Rollie picked up his gear and moved downstream. Before noon he had caught two modest-sized trout, at least big enough to clean and have for lunch. It wasn't anywhere near the ten per day limit, but it was a hell of a lot better than he had done at the other spot. It was the only time on the annual outing when any member of the group had caught the limit, eaten a hearty fish lunch, and could legitimately return to the stream in the afternoon to try again. If the truth were known, it may have been the only time ever, in that stream, when such a feat had been accomplished. Mike never missed the opportunity to remind the Fish Talers of this fact!

Barbara was smiling to herself as she thought about this Fish Taler episode when she noticed Hobie and Janice come through the door. Hobie spotted Barbara, picked her up, swung her around, and planted a big kiss on her cheek. Barbara was equally excited at seeing Hobie and Janice. Both had been classmates of hers during their last years of senior high. Hobie had dated both Janice and Barbara, and a lot of people thought that Barbara and Hobie were serious enough about one another to get married. They, however, had had other ideas. Hobie had planned to become a pharmacist and knew that he had four or five years of school before he could think about marriage. Similarly, Barbara had already made plans to attend an out-of-state school. She had not completely decided upon a major, but was thinking strongly about business. No one in her family, either on her mother's side or her father's, had gone to college, and she would be the first. The family had been in the furniture business for many years, so she thought that a degree in business would be especially good for her, since she had every intention of returning home to learn the business and eventually to take over. Her parents had liked the idea and were very proud of the fact that finally one of the children in the family wanted to continue her schooling.

Janice, as Hobie described her, was a good sport, a good

time at a party—and that she was. Everyone liked her. She always was invited to all the doings; she was the life of the party. She sang, danced, and talked to everyone and kept things lively. You just wouldn't plan a party without having Janice there. No one ever thought that Janice and Hobie were more than good friends, so when they announced their engagement, it came as a surprise to all. Unlike Barbara, Janice skipped school and took a cashier's job at the Super Duper. Hobie attended the University of Northern Iowa at Cedar Falls, and it was during the summer of his second year that the two got married. Everyone expected the obvious in such a hasty marriage, but since they never had any children, all the guesses were wrong. No one really knew why it happened, but it did. The fact that Barbara met Rollie during the first year that she attended St. Olaf's and became engaged the following fall realistically altered whatever hopes Hobie may have had regarding her and perhaps had something to do with strengthening the relationship between Janice and himself. But to this day no one really knew for certain.

"It's great to see you," Hobie said after he let her gently to the floor. "It's been so long" he said, "since we've been together." Actually it was just two years since Barbara and the family were there and Rollie had spent the weekend on the fishing trip.

"Hobie," Barbara said, "you haven't changed at all, still kissing the girls. And Janice, it's so good to see you," and Barbara moved across the room and kissed and hugged her.

"It's wonderful to see you," Janice replied. "I'm sorry that Rollie isn't here. We have such a good time when we're all together," and Janice thought about the good times during the past years. When Barbara and Rollie were in town they partied, and Janice was at her best in those circumstances. But in the past year there had been no celebrating, and it showed in Janice.

"Where's the booze?" shouted Hobie as Mike appeared with a bottle of gin in each hand.

"Want me to mix 'em like in camp," Mike asked, "or would you prefer a more gentle drink?" Mike mixed them very dry—just passing the vermouth quickly over the gin in the hopes that a look at the print on the label would suffice.

"Add a drop or two for me," Hobie replied, for he did like to cut the gin some. And the party started.

By midevening everyone had arrived and it was obvious that all were having a great time. It was a warm August night, and the gin and tonics and martinis were the perfect drinks. Polly had prepared an abundance of hors d'oeuvres (with Barbara's help, of course), and there seemed to be nothing lacking. A few folk huddled around the piano trying to sing some of the new songs Polly had learned to play; others were just wandering around the house, talking here and there with friends, usually about politics. It was the way all successful parties go: you don't remember what made it a success, but it was.

Barbara was sitting on the steps on the back porch when Hobie came through the door.

"It's getting hot in there," he said.

"It's beautiful out here," Barbara answered, and she invited him to stay and talk a while.

"A perfect night," Hobie said. "Not a cloud in the sky. And they said it was going to rain!"

Barbara got up and started to walk toward the pond at the far end of the yard. Hobie followed her. At the north side of the pond, directly in line with the kitchen window, Mike had built a fence, more for looks than any protection it could offer. Barbara cupped her drink in her hands and leaned against the fence. She was looking at the stars and seemed to be deep in thought. Hobie stood next to her and gazed abstractly at things. Then he looked toward the house and the activity inside.

"Have you heard from Rollie?" Hobie asked, feeling uneasy at this point, wanting to talk but not really sure what to say.

"No, I haven't" came her reply. She did not elaborate.

Hobie thought about the times he and Barbara had dated. He wondered whether Barbara was thinking the same thoughts. When he had kissed her earlier, it seemed so natural, and yet he detected a certain chemistry in that brief embrace that he had difficulty forgetting. He silently dropped his glass on the grass and turned to Barbara. She was still filling her lungs with the delicious night air and looking upward toward the stars. Hobie wanted to take Barbara in his arms and hold her; he wanted to kiss her and tell her how much he had missed her. He wanted things to be different; he wanted her. Of course he would not force himself upon her, especially here where at any minute one of the others could discover them—they could even see them quite easily from the house. But no one inside was concerned; the party was going well, and everyone was busy. Besides, why would anyone suspect that after all this time Hobie and Barbara would feel strongly about one another? It was ridiculous to think that way.

"Hold me," Barbara whispered, and he did. Hobie held her hard for a long time. He did not kiss her, but could feel the contour of her lovely body against his; she heightened feelings within him. He wished they had been somewhere else, that they could continue this passion, which had happened so quickly tonight. Hobie was now oblivious to all except Barbara; he did not worry about who would see them or the consequences of their embrace. He felt Barbara begin to shake, so he relaxed some to see if she was all right. Barbara did not speak, but turned from him and looked into the water.

"Is anything the matter?" Hobie asked. He couldn't understand Barbara's abrupt action in pulling away from him.

"Please leave me alone," she said and kept staring at the water.

Hobie picked up the two glasses that were lying on the grass and slowly made his way toward the house. He was not ashamed of what had happened, yet did feel uneasy about walking straight to the house and back to the party. Would his face betray any guilt feelings?

"Have you seen Barbara?" Polly asked. Polly was fixing another dish of munchies at the kitchen counter.

"She's at the pond," Hobie answered, not certain whether the question was in earnest or whether it was Polly's way of letting him know that she had seen what had happened.

"Hey, Barbara," Polly shouted from the door. "I'm putting out the cold trout you wanted. Better hurry, or it'll be gone before you've had a chance to taste any."

Barbara did not answer, but turned and headed for the house. She came through the door, looking refreshed from the night air and seemingly unaffected by what had just happened.

"Is this from the big one?" she said to Hobie, knowing that he had caught a 2½ pounder on the last outing.

"No," interrupted Mike. "We ate that one for dinner. It was the only thing we caught the first day." They never violated their fisherman's vow to eat fish for dinner on opening day or eat nothing. (A few times it was touch and go and the fish dinner was supplemented with a lot of vegetables, potatoes, and gin. But they never faltered on the opening day.)

"It's good," Barbara said and, to her surprise, ate several large pieces. She normally wasn't a fish eater, but this was a tasty meal. "Why does it taste so good?" she asked. "It's not at all like the stuff we used to eat every Friday night back in the abstinence days."

"It's the great Iowa water that does it," chimed in Karl, who by this time had left the piano and had joined the group attempting to make short work of the trout.

Everyone was happy and the party continued as it had for the past several hours. There was more singing and talking, and even the eating continued until midnight. When Polly fixed hor d'oeuvres there was never any reason for dinner! Karl was engaged in some serious discussion with Polly and Janice about the upcoming election and whether or not the Democrats, choosing the relatively unknown Jimmy Carter as their candidate, had done the right thing. Yes, there was general national feeling that Nixon was a scoundrel and, as many on both sides, felt deserved to be imprisoned for what he had done, but already the intensity of the accusations was beginning to wane in the minds of the public.

"I really don't think Ford should have granted him a pardon," said Polly, an avid Democrat and most outspoken about the Republicans and Watergate. "I don't deny that Ford had a great reputation in the Senate, but he hasn't conducted himself with the same sense of responsibility since he has assumed the presidency," she concluded.

"It bothers me," said Janice, "that people are minimizing this whole affair and treating it as though it was just unfortunate that Nixon got caught."

"A lot of politicians feel that way," said Karl, but his point tonight was that the Democrats needed a national figure, another John Kennedy, to lead the nation and establish that charisma that had been absent during the past administration. "But I don't want to see Ted in there either," he said. "They'd just kill him." They all agreed.

When Karl and Paula said good-bye, it was two-thirty, and that signalled the end of the party. They were always the last to leave. Mike and Polly picked up a bit, but left much of the mess for the morning.

Mike was on vacation for a few days, so there would be no rush in the morning. Everyone could sleep in.

Barbara was sitting on the sofa sipping the remnant of a martini fixed sometime earlier. Mike and Polly said good night and went upstairs to their bedroom. Barbara was staying in the spare room to the left of the kitchen, one Mike had just recently remodeled and enlarged. It used to be a large hall closet, and when he put the extension on the back of the house it had been an easy matter to make the closet into a more useful room. They had never used it for anything except to throw a lot of junk into it, and they did need another room. So, it was converted. Barbara mused about the evening and eventually wondered about Rollie and how he was getting along. She understood that he may not have thought to send a card the first week, forgetting that mail from Ireland, even when there is no postal strike, takes over a week to reach the States. When they were there in '74, they sent cards to everyone during their second week, and Rollie was in the backyard, home for two days, talking to a neighbor when the mailman delivered a card sent nine days earlier. It always happened that way.

It was now quarter to three, and all the children were sleeping. Barbara got up and went into her room. In a very short time, she was asleep, able to put the night's activities completely out of her mind. She had no thoughts of eating or drinking; nor did she even once recall what had happened at the pond. Hobie, on the other hand, remembered vividly what had occurred.

Janice and Hobie had left the party close to one because Janice was feeling the effects of the drink. She was not sick, but felt a little giddy, she explained to Polly when they left. They lived only a few blocks from Mike and Polly, so they were home within a very short time. Once in bed, Hobie and Janice made love. It was then that Hobie recalled all that had happened and how he had so wanted to lie with Barbara. He closed his eyes and pretended Janice was she, and however he dreamed, it had no adverse affect upon Janice. She loved Hobie and was still thrilled every time they made love to one another. She felt so happy that Hobie had married her. He was the perfect husband, never forgetting a birthday or anniversary and always being there when she needed him most. Hobie realized tonight that he did not feel the same way about Janice; their marriage had been a mistake. He had fought these feelings for years, convincing himself that it was possible to love anyone—if you tried hard enough. Any couple can make a marriage work. This marriage did work, but not to his satisfaction. Tonight, when he should be pleased with his wife, he couldn't wait to get finished and go to sleep. He wanted Barbara, not Janice. He was determined to have his way.

CHAPTER FIVE

Rollie would have no way of knowing, but at the same time that Barbara was enjoying herself at the country club, he had just walked into the dining room at Mrs. Malone's for breakfast, the first one at her place since he had arrived. Altough he had left his things in the room on Monday afternoon and had accepted the gracious hospitality and concern of both Mrs. Malone and Mr. Malone that evening, it was not until this Wednesday morning that he was able to take a meal at the house. Rollie reasoned that it must have been something he had eaten that made him sick, but whatever it was, it proved to be too much to overcome with a night's rest. All of Tuesday he lay in bed, head reeling and stomach upset; he had little inclination to turn over, much less attempt to take any nourishment. Mrs. Malone looked in on him every couple of hours, but soon realized that his groaning was more habit than an indication of anything serious. At one point, she did consider calling the doctor, but when she checked on Rollie for about the fifth time that day, his color had returned and he was able to smile and talk much more coherently. Rollie would not believe it was a hangover; it just had to be food poisoning.

This morning, Rollie met the "Germans" for the first time. He found them delightful people, Karl and Helga and their two children, Ron and Bard. Only Karl was able to speak English, and he did so quite well. The mystery about the "Germans" was solved at breakfast when Rollie learned that Mrs. Malone just refused to try and pronounce the name Henschmeidt and simply preferred to identify the family by referring to their nationality. Rollie was certain that Mrs. Malone was oblivious to any possible insult that might have been associated with persons who are addressed by anything but their proper names. And it was quite evident from both the environment and the tenor of the conversation that the Henschmeidts took no offense.

The daylong sleep cure had apparently worked well, for Rollie had no ill effects from Monday's misfortunes. Tuesday had been lost, but Wednesday still held the possibility of greatness. It was a brilliantly sunny day—and warm—and Rollie hoped that the fishing would be excellent. The Henschmeidts were going to play golf and asked if Rollie would care to join them. He thanked them, but declined the invitation. Golf he could play anytime and mostly did; fishing in the Shannon River was only possible on very rare occasions. Barbara would have been proud of his decision.

Rollie didn't worry about a taxi this morning, but hurried down the walk to the street, turned left, and headed into town, almost at a trot. Within fifteen minutes, he was at Mr. McDougal's house, and just in time to find him at home. Had he been fifteen minutes later, McDougal would have been off on his own fishing expedition.

At this point, Rollie suddenly remembered that he was supposed to have appeared the previous day at nine o'clock. It embarrassed him to think that he could so easily have forgotten that, but still he did not want to miss this chance to fish the Shannon. He introduced himself to Mr. McDougal and apologized to him for not appearing on the previous day. McDougal seemed not at all disturbed by the whole thing, so Rollie proceeded to the important issue. He asked about a boat and learned that one of those old large and rough-looking but sturdy rowboats rented for five pounds for the day; tackle, such that it was, brought the total to seven pounds. Rollie was so intent upon fishing that he didn't stop to figure out that McDougal was asking about seventeen or eighteen dollars for the outfit, probably just a bit too much. But fishing in the Shannon was impossible without boat and tackle, so Rollie took him up on the offer. McDougal pointed out a good spot, shoved him off, and the fishing got underway.

No sooner had Rollie rowed to the exact spot, which had been pointed out to him, than it began to rain. He was very surprised, since his last glance at the sky had revealed only blue. Now it was extremely cloudy, and it appeared as though he was in for a good wetting. He determined not to become disillusioned. Checking the lure (rusted on one side) and trying the line, he cast a scant twenty feet from the boat. Aside from the knots at that point in the line, he snagged a piece of driftwood and cut his hand on one of the oar locks when the sudden jerk of the line almost pulled the pole from his grasp. He cursed the maneuver, drew the line, untangled it, loosed the hook from the log, and tried again.

The sun began to shine. Perhaps it was a test, he thought, and he proved much more successful on this second try. Rollie artfully drew the lure through the water, just a foot from the surface, and hooked a large pickerel. Anyone who fishes knows the feeling of a good hit, and Rollie was full of that feeling. Rain or shine would make no difference; the fish was all that mattered now. He played it for a bit, and then his excitement got the better of him and he started to reel the line in rapidly. When the fish drew alongside the boat, Rollie gave a snap of his line and the fish landed at his feet. It had large teeth—as pickerel do—so Rollie was careful not to grab at it from underneath. He put his left foot over the middle of its body and pressed firmly enough so that the fish remained motionless. (One shouldn't be fooled by such a fish ploy, for Rollie remembered the time he put one of these sturdy pickerels in the trunk of his car, went off to lunch, returned an hour later, thinking that this fish was not the right size, and was very surprised to see it revive itself and swim away once he had replaced it in the water.) Through the excitement of the prospect of fishing in the river Shannon, Rollie had neglected either to obtain a landing net—not too serious a problem—or to secure a pliers with which to disengage the hook. He also did not have a stringer. When the pickerel started moving and managed to free itself from both Rollie's foothold and its hook, it didn't know what a great favor it had done Rollie. With a quick lift of the toe of his shoe, Rollie sent the pickerel back to the depths from which it came.

The morning went quickly, and although Rollie had caught

but two more fish, one a very small perch and another an even smaller "something else," he pulled his craft to the dock and looked forward to a good lunch so that he could resume fishing in the afternoon. After that initial downpour, the sun had shone all morning. It quickly dried Rollie's clothes and soothed his temperament so that the pleasure of fishing was as pronounced here as it would have been with the Fish Talers from Iowa.

It was well after noon, so Rollie wasted little time hurrying down the road to the first restaurant he could find. He hoped that he would not reenact the episode of '74, when all of the restaurants he tried one day had closed for lunch! He was in luck. Claery's was open. He went inside and walked past the pastry shop and up several steps to the back room and the dining area. He found an unoccupied table in the corner, sat down and ordered three scones and a pot of tea. (He remembered about the coffee.) He loved Irish scones, and he once thought that a steady diet of them should keep a man's disposition cheery forever. He did not care at all for most Irish cuisine (except, of course, for breakfast), but the scones, he believed, were sent from heaven. He was also convinced that they were made especially to be eaten with tea, since tea never appealed to him unless he was eating scones. Lunch had pleased him so much that he ordered three "to go" and smuggled four pats of butter into the bag and carried them off to resume his fishing holiday. He even thought twice about buying a bottle of claret to take along, but then decided against it because he didn't have a corkscrew readily at hand.

The afternoon dragged; the sun continued to shine, but the fish refused to bite. No matter where he moved the boat, he could find no success. After a few hours, he couldn't even find his original spot, and he was certain that if he could locate it he would have the same good fortune that he had had in the morning. But he just could not find it. When things go wrong, they really go wrong. He also lost two scones when he stood up in the boat and the bag slipped from his pocket and fell into the water. He managed to grab it, but only one scone was worth saving; the others had soaked through. The butter, too, presented problems. It had melted in his pocket, and although it did not seep through the wrappings, it was impossible to spread on the remaining scone. He ate the scone dry, but did not enjoy it. It simply did not taste as good as he imagined it would.

He rowed the boat back to the dock, but found he could not get the boat close enough to it so he could step off. He had forgotten about the tide, and now the level had gone down so much that the dock stood fully six feet from as near as he could work the boat. Fortunately, he was able to avoid wet feet by tying the boat to one adjacent and carefully stepping from one boat to another until he reached the shore. In all, it had not been a bad day, but it did leave him in a nasty frame of mind, considering how marvelous things had been earlier in the day. He took the oars and tackle back to McDougal's front porch and headed for Mrs. Malone's.

As Rollie passed Claery's on his way back, he wondered why he was headed back to his room. He had not intended to take high tea with the Malone's and he definitely did not want a repeat of Monday at the Prince of Wales. He turned into Claery's with the thought that some bread, cheese, and wine might do just fine. He first moved his way though the crowd at the bakery counter, as he decided it was wiser to get his bread first; the wine would be there later. Luckily, he managed to purchase the last loaf of Italian bread on the shelf, and this pleased him almost as much as if it had been the purchase of the last available scones. To go with the bread, he did, in fact, purchase a few scones. They would be an excellent dessert. He left the crowded counter and moved to a short line on the opposite side of the store, waited patiently for two ladies to taste a variety of cheeses, and then picked out what he believed to be a mild cheddar, or a cheese that at least tasted like cheddar, and bought half a pound. Since the wine was also ordered at this location, he picked out a French ordinaire, paid for both items, gathered his bags together, and headed for a bench just on the other side of the bridge in a lovely little park that sat on the east side of the Shannon. The bench was a little dusty, so he spread out a newspaper, which someone had left in the corner, and sat down. It didn't occur to him that after having spent all day in a boat, which was perceivably much more dusty than the bench, his pants really didn't need the protection he was giving them. But dinner was at hand, and such thoughts were not likely to enter his mind.

As content as he had been eating the scones at lunch, this adventure tonight surpassed even that. He had had the foresight to ask Claery's to uncork the wine before he had left the store, so it presented no problem. He tore off a chunk of bread, broke a piece of cheese, and put the two together to make a delicious sandwich. He swigged the wine generously, and before long he was completely relaxed and content. Boats were moving up and down the river—some people partying on them, others arguing, and some just motoring along, seemingly unaware of anyone or anything around them. Rollie studied human nature and marveled at how much you could learn just through this simple observation. If he hadn't been abruptly brought back to the realization of where he was by the sudden downpour (as so often occurred in Ireland), he might have sat there until dark. But the experience was so refreshing to him that he was not in the least upset by the rain and apologized to Mrs. Malone with a smile on his face, as he tried to move quickly through the hall to his room so that he might not soil the rug with the dirt he had tracked into the house. It was one of the few smiles Mrs. Malone had seen on Rollie in the past two days.

Rollie went to bed early and slept soundly. A full day on the river had made him more exhausted than he had realized, and sleep came quickly. He dreamed of a marvelous tomorrow.

☆ ☆ ☆

Rollie waved good-bye and lifted his bags into the taxi for the short ride to the station. He planned to catch the 10:00 A.M. train west, because he wanted to be in Galway before dark. Had he waited until the next train, it would have taken until nine-thirty that evening, and he decided it would have been impossible either to find a car rental shop open or to make his way to St. Joseph's on St. Mary's Road. Mrs. Malone was sad that he should leave Athlone so soon; she was beginning to treat him like her son. (Rollie suspected that any visitor who stayed more than a day would have been treated similarly. Mrs. Malone loved her visitors.) There was no question that Mrs. Malone's accommodations were among the best Rollie had taken in Ireland, but he reasoned that Athlone, aside from the Shannon, had little interest for him. Already he was into his fourth day and it seemed that time was passing much too quickly. Rollie thanked Mrs. Malone for all that she had done; this morning, he was especially pleased with the little packet of goodies she had provided for the trip. Nine pounds a day and all the extras was a very good deal, he thought. So dedicated was Mrs. Malone to making her guests feel comfortable and pleased with their stay, that breakfast might consist of the usual, plus cakes, Irish pudding, and a variety of pancakes—the kind one seldom sees in Ireland except on Shrove Tuesday. Even Mr. Malone was outside that Thursday morning, and Rollie had not seen or heard from him since that first meeting on Monday evening. A lot had happened since then.

Rollie got more attention at the station than he expected. A porter was present to carry bags to the platform, and two ticket windows were open to serve the travelers. Only two passengers purchased tickets for the westbound train, so Rollie wondered why the change from Monday. Perhaps they were preparing for the weekend and the Dublin horse show, when the number of people going to Dublin becomes significantly larger than at any other time during the year. As a matter of fact, the thought of the horse show brought a sudden pang to Rollie; he had planned to spend at least one day at Phoenix Park learning something about the sport. He thought now that it was improbable that he would have the time or the inclination to return to the east coast so soon. He had better make the most of Galway, otherwise he'd have another part of his trip over which to anguish. This "travel as the spirit moves you" might not prove to be as satisfying as he had imagined.

The fifty-eight–mile trip from Athlone to Galway was relatively uneventful except for the several stops long the way where Rollie witnessed motley groups of natives, caravans, milk carts, and the like, all of which, from time to time, seemed to have some hold over the train, which apparently made the engineer vary the speed frequently. The greatest impression a visitor has as he approaches the west coast is the gradual build up of the stone fences that divide the parcels of land. Rollie watched one line of stone fences, which ran perpendicular to other stone fences and seemingly sectioned off the land into what appeared to be four- or five-acre squares, for over fifteen minutes before he saw a break in the line. He wondered how long it had taken to build that row and how the builder had managed to keep it in what seemed to be such a straight line. He began to understand why the Irish were forced to import so much foodstuff as he observed mile after mile of rocky land, fit only for sheep and goat grazing. Even cattle would have found it difficult to get much nourishment from these pastures. In all his travel in Ireland, including the '74 trip, Rollie had yet to see one cow or pig! He reasoned that the pigs could be kept out of sight, but how does one hide cows?

The train on which Rollie was riding was fairly comfortable. It did not have the cushioned seats such as one would find in the American trains, but it did have that characteristic European closed compartment, even for day riders. It was a pleasure for Rollie to be able to close the door, which effectively kept the smoke from the rest of the train out of that compartment. Ever since Rollie had given up smoking over ten years before, it bothered him to be forced to endure smoke, particularly in a public conveyance. (It didn't seem to have any adverse effects in bars, however. Smokers refer to this phenomenon as the non-S syndrome, and, depending upon the magnanimity of the labeler, "non-S" can be interpreted as "nonsmoker" or "nonsense syndrome." Rollie never welcomed any reference to this touchy issue.)

The train arrived at the Galway station about an hour after noon, as far as Rollie could remember. There had been some confusion as he reached the platform in the station, and it took several minutes before he could work his way through the crowd and find the exit. At first, he found himself at the door to the hotel that adjoined the station. When he realized where he was, he turned and walked in the opposite direction, went through the door of the ticket office, and discovered it had no exit to the street outside. Finally he found several doors to the street—through a second ticket office—and walked to the edge of the road. He made inquiries about the location of Bord Failte and eventually dragged his bags the relatively short distance to that office. There was the usual confusion and noise in the office and the mixture of English- and non–English-speaking people that by now Rollie had grown accustomed to seeing in these offices. He secured a room reservation at St. Joseph's on St. Mary's Road, just seven blocks from downtown Galway, and felt most fortunate to have managed it. This was the week of races in Galway, and many Irishmen had taken holidays (and rooms) in the city. Rollie experienced little difficulty in hiring a taxi and set out for St. Joseph's.

St. Joseph's was no more than a fifteen-minute walk from the Galway market and city center, so Rollie would be able to get around town quite easily without a car. However, once he had become situated in his room, understood the procedure for meals, and had familiarized himself with the whereabouts of the bathroom, kitchen, and lounge, he set out on foot to explore the area in Ireland with which, as a result of his '74 trip, he had become most familiar. He judged that should he stay several days in Galway, this path to the downtown area would become second nature, if not well worn. His intention today was to rent a car, once again, with the hopes that the investment made this time would be decidedly wiser than a similar decision made at Shannon, where the sole use of the vehicle turned out to be a rather expensive means of getting from the airport to Dublin. He was certain that the problems of congestion and heavy traffic would not be nearly so pronounced here as they had been in Dublin. But, Rollie never made it to the rental office.

"How many do you think are out there?" Rollie asked, never recalling having seen such an impressive number of wild birds.

" 'Tousans," came the reply. Rollie thought immediately the gentleman used linguistic license with the answer, yet after having begun to count the birds, he himself would have believed there were thousands down in the water.

"Are these swans here all of the time," Rollie asked, "or do they migrate at a certain time of the year?" He somehow thought the old gentleman, clutching his bottle, would know the answer to his question.

"They never leave—except to move a bit on downstream in the afternoon," he said.

There were, if not thousands, hundreds of white mute swans decorating the shores of the river Carrib, just beneath O'Brien's Bridge. The sight was breathtaking, especially if one had never had occasion to see such large fowl and in such impressive numbers. The whiteness of the birds made it seem as though large patches of white flowers were drifting along the edge of the river, and the presence of the cathedral in the background completed the picture of a century-old Camelot; it was like being in another age. Rollie riveted himself to the spot and paid no attention to traffic and passersby. This also made him forget his purpose, this afternoon, in walking to the city. By now the rental offices were closed, so he must wait until another day.

He peered harder into the water and discovered unbelievable schools of fish, trout and salmon. It looked as though one need only to drop a line, baited or not, into the water and, just because of the sheer numbers of fish, catch something. It seemed that obvious to others as well, since there were a number of gentleman fisherman along the banks trying to attract these fish—without success. For the full hour and a half that he stood watching, he did not witness a single catch. However much Rollie longed to have a pole and begin again what he had started in the Shannon, he realized that if these waters yielded the fish he thought they should, some real fishermen would be about; and he saw none. It was all for show, and the fish knew it. Imagine, if you will, thousands of five-to-eight-pounders scurrying about in the water and no one able to do anything but look. Rollie's fisherman sense imagined it was nature's way of paying back those squanderers of nature's gifts, those unsportsmanlike anglers who plundered the deep with no intention of using the catch for food. Rollie thought it ironic that a land with such plenty in its waters should ever have gone hungry. If ever he had opportunity to talk literature with Anna again, he would make this point while discussing the Macken trilogy. It was the first time in several days that Anna Barton had entered his mind.

CHAPTER SIX

It had not taken Rollie all afternoon to get to O'Brien's Bridge. When he left St. Joseph's and turned right on Shantallow Road, he stopped at a meat market. There was nothing unusual about this meat market, except that the doors were open to the street, from where you could see sides of beef, loins of pork, and legs of lamb hanging over the various cutting blocks behind the counter; the showcases—without glass covers—were filled with cleaned chickens. The shop was not air-conditioned, and no one seemed at all concerned about the flies that swarmed about the meat. Rollie wanted to go inside the store and tell them about refrigeration, but he didn't. He just shook his head and moved on.

As he walked along Shantallow toward St. Dominick Street, he noticed the bottles of milk that stood beside the stone steps of a number of houses along the street. He thought it strange, since it was now well after noon and he judged the milk had been delivered early in the day. Rollie stood for a moment and looked up and down the street, trying to figure out what it was that made things look different. Then it dawned on him: there was no grass anywhere, only sidewalk and street. Yet only a block back and around the corner of St. Mary's Road, you could see large gardens in the front of all the houses and even larger expanses of land directly across the street from those residences. *What constrasts!* he thought, *in such a small area.*

When Rollie finally reached St. Dominick Street, he remembered that the Claddagh Quay was nearby, and he turned to head toward what he thought was the inlet from the bay. His sense of direction was not quite correct, but within ten minutes he did spot the quay and hurried to see if any boats were lying on their sides because of low tide. He was not disappointed.

There were several large fishing boats listing in shallow water, and as he looked at the rubbish, so visible in the muddy bottom of the bay, he marveled at how high tide would bring back the beauty and serenity of this wonderful place. *Strange,* he thought, *that the attractiveness of this scene should be so dependent upon the whim of nature.* It was after this experience that Rollie proceeded to O'Brien Bridge, where he spent an additional couple of hours observing nature and breathing in the beauty of his surroundings.

Rollie had not eaten since his breakfast at Mrs. Malone's, and now he was hungry. It was about five-thirty, so Rollie wandered toward the center of town to the general area of the little park across from the Great Southern Hotel. When he arrived near the park, he spotted what seemed to be an attractive restaurant called the Odeon. He looked through the window and saw people eating, so he went inside. Although he had been in Galway once before, he had never gone into a hotel lobby and dining room to eat, so the procedure here fascinated him. He went to the desk clerk to make inquiries about dinner and was handed a menu and asked to place his order. He chose an egg salad sandwich (which he knew would be served dry unless he specifically asked for butter and mayonnaise), two scones, tea, and pastry. He asked whether or not he should seat himself in the dining room or lobby, and the clerk told him to sit anywhere that was comfortable. Rollie walked to the dining room and sat down. In a few minutes, a pretty young girl came with his order; the room was crowded, and many people had not yet been served. Rollie wondered how she knew that it was his order, but he was hungry and decided against asking her, for fear that it may not have been his order. He devoured his food, scones and all, and felt satisfied. As he got up to leave, he thought about the terrible Wimpy's Restaurants he had frequented so often on his last trip and how the grease had clung to his innards for the whole trip. No grease here and at a most reasonable price of seventy pence. Ireland was heaven!

This day had started out well and had become even better as the day wore on. Rollie loved this charming hotel with its strange customs and people who chose to eat their sandwiches in so many places; he wondered if American hotels might adopt the practice of encouraging customers to order at the hotel desk and sit wherever they wanted, lobby or dining room. And how many frustrated waitresses would there be, frantically searching about for their diners. This called for a lager, and he headed for the bar.

It took Rollie several bar outings during his '74 trip to discover what one calls the lighter beer served in Ireland. He liked the dark beer and stout well enough, but he could not drink much of either. Lager was what he wanted, preferably refrigerated. Room-temperature stout did not treat him kindly. Rollie was glad that he could now get the beer he wanted, and as he sat sipping and aimlessly gazing out the front window of the Odeon bar, he thought of Anna. He wondered what she was doing, whether she and Jack were together, what she had planned for the evening, and if she remembered him.

Rollie got up from his seat at the window and headed for the telephone in the lobby. He "rang up" Anna without any trouble; he had finally learned the proper use of the phone.

"How wonderful to hear from you. How have you been?" asked Anna on the other end of the line.

"Things have gone well," Rollie answered, "except for fishing in the Shannon. All I caught was a cold!"

"Where are you now?" she asked.

"Sitting here in the Odeon Hotel lobby," he answered without hesitation. It was thrilling to hear her voice and to detect, he thought, an excitement in her voice as she spoke to him.

"I saw James a few days ago, and he and Patricia will leave tomorrow for holidays in Rome. It really sounds like they will have a great time." She sounded as excited about that news as she did about the call from him, and that bothered him.

"I wish all of you were here now; the weather has been great." He said all of you, but Rollie had no interest, at least today, in seeing anyone but Anna. "Do you have any plans for a short vacation yet this summer?" Rollie continued.

"Oh, Jack and I spent three wonderful days in Cork. We

just returned. I hadn't been in the house more than ten minutes when you called." This answer momentarily stunned Rollie. He did not like to hear about Anna and Jack.

"I thought Jack went by himself," Rollie said.

"Well, he did, but I received a call on Sunday that relieved me of that job responsibility, so I decided to rush off to Cork. Jack and I always stay at the same place, so I knew it would be easy to find him." Anna spoke so freely about this relationship that Rollie began to feel uneasy.

"I hope you had a good time," Rollie felt compelled to say.

"Oh, we had a marvelous time, one party after another. Jack got that new account, and it should mean some rather impressive profits." This news further depressed Rollie. He had felt so good all day, and now this. He wished that he had never placed the call.

"I plan to be back in Dublin in about a week, at least for a day, before I leave for London," Rollie said. "I hope we can get together for a drink or something."

"Let's plan on it," she said. "James won't be here, but I'm certain that Myra will join the three of us." She just wouldn't let go of Jack.

"Well, then, I'll call on Wednesday or Thursday and we'll see what happens," he said. Why worry about Anna until then?

"Thanks for calling. We'll look forward to Wednesday, then," Anna continued to include the unwanted guest.

Rollie returned to the bar and ordered another lager, changed his mind, and asked for some Paddy. He sat down at the booth and reviewed all that had happened since he had arrived in Ireland. He realized that he had no claim on Anna, that, in fact he should not even have been thinking about her. She had been introduced to him on Saturday night at Connolly's and just happened to be someone who was pleased to talk with him. He should have been no more disillusioned with her attraction to Jack than he was with Pat's relationship with James. He had intended to take this trip to visit places and things he had seen only briefly on the '74 trip, and he wanted to do it without having to look after his children. To some extent, he was accomplishing that goal, but Anna was totally unexpected and really unwanted. But he could not deny that a relationship was beginning to grow.

The Paddy tasted good, so he ordered another. He rested his head upon the leather back of the booth and thought about the land, especially as his favorite Irish author, Walter Macken, had described it in *Rain on the Wind:* "High over them the sun was shining brightly—shining on calm waters of the Bay to one side of them and on the green grass under them, and glinting blindingly off the rows of the whitewashed thatched cottages with here and there the brown nets slung on the pegs driven into the walls. It was a grand scene that would have been very peaceful indeed if it wasn't for the gander. . . . " Macken had rekindled within Rollie the urgency to see, once again, the beautiful sights of the West, the hills, lakes, ancient ruins and abbeys, the jagged coast, and the unchanged miles of countryside, seemingly the same today as it had been two hundred years before. There was a beauty in this rocky land, he thought, that is unique. It was a kind of granite greenness that yields to no man, but remains for all to enjoy. Each turn in the road produced a new scene that might well serve the hordes of neophyte artists the perfect landscape on which to work. He thought of Mico Mor, standing there in his red petticoat, unaware of any ridicule directed toward him—innocence at its height, and a spirit unchanged, even in adulthood, as Rollie pictured the young man Mico, twenty years later, struggling with the giant waves in his small boat, certain suicide for most men, except for Mico himself. As he had conquered the problems of his youth, so would he, Mico, be victorious over the trials of later life. And as Macken concludes his novel, Mico sights land and the frantic viewers standing on the quay in disbelief:

> He saw Twacky.
> O God, I hit Twacky!
> I love Twacky! I'll marry Twacky!
> And he leaned over and patted the leaping boat on her rough side.

"You're a great oul bitch!" he said aloud. "You're a great oul beautiful black bitch."

And Rollie transported himself to the beauty and glory of another time.

Rollie sighed as though reaching a catharsis. He was satiated with an overwhelming love for this land, this Ireland, which only now was beginning to have meaning for him, as it had for countless others who would die rather than leave their native land. He was not a native, but he would like to have been. He could not understand why his own father, born and raised in Dublin, never expressed the slightest interest in even visiting his homeland. "I am an American, not an Irishman," Desmond had told his son often. "When I left home it was for good." And he stood by that statement. Desmond deplored the Hibernians who weekly, at their numerous clubs, vicariously relived the joys of the Emerald Isle. "If they like it so much," he would say, "why don't they go back?" and somehow the thought always rang true to Rollie, as he imagined these American foreigners taking jobs away from the real Americans. How could these people continue to remind others about how great the Old Country was and that America could not compare with it? Back then, Rollie had understood what his father had meant. Today, however, he felt differently. He knew the benefits of America and he loved his home, but he also yearned for the simplicity of this land where no one was in a hurry, where the sun rose and fell on each day, one the same as the next, and nothing seemed to change. He could believe the saying that at the end of the world, the Emerald Island would simply sink beneath the sea and not suffer the indignity of holocaust, fire, and destruction. The skirmishes in Belfast alluded to a different theme, but that could be explained, he thought.

Rollie wriggled out of his comfortable seat by the window, bid good-bye to the bartender, and headed for St. Joseph's. It was about nine o'clock, and the players were out on the streets. As he headed down Merchants Road in the general direction of the quay, he saw two different tin-whistle–and-shallow-drum groups. Small crowds listened, often tossing coins to the musicians after each number. As he approached each group, Rollie would stop and listen for a minute and then move on. He was not fond of the tin whistle. Before long he had crossed O'Brien's Bridge and had swung around the corner and started up St. Dominick's toward Shantallow. There was some loud singing coming from the Green Inn Bar, so he went inside. He stood for a moment or two to survey the situation, then walked to the bar and ordered a Paddy. Two young men, obviously full of spirits, were trying to lead a group of five or six sitting in a side booth in some stirring Irish songs. They seemed to be enjoying themselves, and despite the large number of people in the place who were not at all interested in singing, the bartender made no attempt to quiet them. Rollie listened to the songs they were singing, and he could tell right away they were Americans, singing the favorites: "Danny Boy," "Mother Machree," and other Bing Crosby specialties. One fellow saw him and coaxed him to join in, which Rollie did. He spilled a bit of his drink on one of the singers, but it made no difference. Rollie sang with vigor, believing that this was one of those traditional Irish pub singing affairs. (If he had only reflected just momentarily upon his original identification of the singers, he would have been embarrassed to know that he had reached such a conclusion, but . . .) Rollie was very loud, and one of the patrons, sitting at a table beside the door and nearest to Rollie politely asked him to stop singing so loudly. His singing colleagues heard the request and stopped immediately. The men at the table were Irishmen, probably fishermen, and were not happy with the intrustion of these Americans. Quite often such situations cause fights to erupt, but not this time. And Rollie was relieved; he had not gone on vacation to break a nose or jaw, or land in jail. The drinking continued, but the singing was over for the night.

Rollie finished his drink and went out. He continued toward St. Joseph's and soon arrived without benefit of more detours. The front door was slightly ajar, so he did not use his key to enter. He bid good evening to Mrs. Costello, the proprietor, who was standing just outside her living room, where the television was playing, and climbed one flight of stairs to his room. The bathroom was just outside his room, so he did not have any distance to travel (especially on a cold morning) for his morning shower, and he was very happy with such an arrangement. There was a sink in his room, so he had no need for bathroom use that night; he could wash up and brush his teeth in his room.

It was only slightly after ten-thirty, so Rollie could get a good night's sleep. He lay in bed thinking about the day and was generally pleased with what he had done. He had not become too morose over his talk with Anna—at least, he could now think about it without having it ruin his day. Actually, he had talked with her for a much longer time than he had intended. She told him about the day she and Jack spent at Bantry Bay and how they drove for supper to Glengariff and almost ran the rented car off the road as they encountered fog on the way back. She told him about the delicious dinner they had had the first night, one that had compared favorably with the dinner on Sunday at Snaffles, and she recounted the places they saw on the return trip, actually preferring to drive the rented car to Dublin rather than take the train, and suggested that he, Rollie, make provision to visit a number of those places if time permitted. In all, he thought, it wasn't as bad a conversation as he had first imagined, and the good feeling it gave him aided in his near-immediate dropping off to sleep. How wonderful to sleep with good feelings, and that feeling would stay with Rollie for days to come.

CHAPTER SEVEN

Rollie slept longer than usual this morning, so when he had finished washing his hands and face and giving a quick brush to his teeth, he hurried downstairs in order to get some breakfast. *Of all the meals in the day,* he thought, *I don't want to miss breakfast.* Mrs. Costello had already set the tables with clean dishes for dinner, but had kept the one in the corner, the single, still set for breakfast. She knew Rollie would want to eat and would be disappointed if he had not been able to get his eggs, sausage, and soda bread—toasted! It was one attribute that all of these B and B proprietors had in common: they never became impatient with the customers at mealtime. No matter what the situation—or time—one could always get something to eat without complaints (and most of the time without charge) from the management. That was not nearly so true in the hotels, but even there the atmosphere in the dining rooms was always pleasant.

Rollie finished a large breakfast this morning, including the cornflakes and juice, and felt as though it would last him throughout the day. He glanced outside as he started up the stairs and saw the sun. It would be another beautiful day. His goal today was to go immediately to the Budget Rent-a-Car to arrange for a five-day rental, which he judged would be sufficient. He planned to be in Dublin on Wednesday, so five days would give him plenty of time. He would leave Dublin on Thursday and spend the next two days in London. He was already booked to leave London Heathrow on Sunday, so he must be there. If need be, he could make a change in his schedule, but he did that on the '74 trip and the family was lucky to get home when they did. Air Lingus recorded the change all right, but Pan American in Paris had no record of the change. He never discovered who had been negligent and once the family had arrived safely in the United States, it seemed senseless to pursue the matter. It was fortunate that room was available on that flight from Paris.

Rollie finished showering, dressed hurriedly, and rushed down the stairs. He asked Mrs. Costello if it would be all right to leave his bags in the room until he could return with the car; he would be back in less than an hour. He planned to leave Galway around noon, so there would be plenty of time for her to inspect the room after he had gone. He suggested that she might want to change the linen while he was after the car, since he would not need to use the room on his return. There would be no problem, she assured him.

It didn't take Rollie long to get downtown; he glanced at the swans as he passed over the bridge, but this time he did not stop. He hurried through the streets, now teeming with shopping tourists, to the car rental on Eyre Square. Several customers were waiting in the office when he arrived, and he momentarily felt a twinge of despair, a brief moment of anxiety. What if he could not get a car? No, that couldn't happen. He had judged correctly, but only by a chance. If it had not been for the fact that one of the people standing in the office had reserved an automatic, Rollie would have been without a car. The gentleman was explaining that he could not drive a standard and that the agency had assured him an automatic would be available. After having made his reservation several weeks in advance, he simply could not understand why the car was not there. The agent tried to explain that the promised vehicle had been in an accident and that the replacement from Dublin had not yet arrived. It was expected this afternoon, but there was no guarantee. He was very sorry and offered the car that was available—his standard spare—but really could do nothing for him until another automatic arrived.

Rollie balked somewhat at the rental price of seventy-eight pounds, but in view of the situation he thought it best to accept; some car was by far better than none. It was a little larger than he needed or wanted, but it was the only one available. He concluded his business and headed for St. Joseph's. Driving was much easier in Galway than in Dublin except for the drive through the one very narrow section of town near the cathedral. Once past that spot, however, there was very little to hinder his speedy ride to Mrs. Costello's. He parked just outside the front door on St. Mary's, seeing no need to pull into the driveway by the side of the house. There were few cars on the street, and he would only take a minute or two to collect his things and be on his way. He had not yet determined where he would go, but there were several choices. He would like to visit the Aran Islands and stop at Balentubber Abbey en route. He could head south to Limerick and stop at the Cliffs of Moher on the way, or he might head straight for the Dingle Peninsula and hope to have sufficient light through the Connor Pass so that he could once again take in the beauty of Ireland from the mountains. These things were running through his head as he thanked Mrs. Costello for the room and wonderful breakfasts. She hoped he would come again, and she wished him a safe journey, wherever he was headed. She could not understand this American who, unlike others she had known, had little use for tourist buses and guides. She did not realize how well Rollie knew his way around, not only as a result of his '74 trip, when he had felt completely unsure of himself, but because of the intense study he had done in the intervening years, going over in his mind—and on the maps—all aspects of his first visit, even to the smallest detail of street names, hotels and restaurants, routes, and even the shops in some of the most remote sections of the country. For a foreigner who had spent only a few weeks in the country two years before, Rollie demonstrated a remarkable knowledge of people and places in Ireland. It was true that he still had some misgivings about Dublin, but the East Coast was not his favorite part of Ireland. He loved the West, and he knew it thoroughly. And by now he knew, too, that he would forsake a second visit to Balentubber for the thrill of the ride through Connor Pass. He knew it would take no more than two and a half hours to Limerick and probably three more to the pass. Since it was barely noon at this moment, he thought he would be at the pass before six, and that would be perfect. However, Rollie had not considered that today was Friday and that traffic in Limerick would be heavy. Shannon as a busy day on Saturday, and most tourists spent Friday night in Limerick so they would be nearby for the next day's trip. Besides, the natives in the area would have reached the end of another workweek, and the drinking started in early afternoon in downtown Limerick. Crossing Sarsfield Bridge would be near impossible if he did not arrive before two o'clock.

As Rollie pulled away from St. Joseph's, he realized he was headed in the wrong direction. When he got to the corner, he took a left turn on Crescent and doubled back on William until he reached St. Dominick. The traffic was beginning to get heavy now in Galway, and it took much longer for him to reach Eyre Square and move on to Forster than he had planned. Although even heavy traffic should not have held him up too much, there had been an accident between a delivery truck and a bakery truck and the narrow street through which he must pass was blocked. He waited fully forty-five minutes before the situation was eased, and even then the cars could barely crawl through the town. It was one-thirty before he reached the highway and was on his way.

Rollie drove through the countryside, unhampered by the obstacles he had found in Galway. He drove west on Route N6 until he got to Athenry, where he turned south on N18, now firmly on his way to Limerick. About one and a half hours from the time he had left Galway, he was in Ennis, and he smiled some when he thought of his past experience in Ennis, dining in the Beehive Cafe. This time he did not stop; nor would he ever dine at the Beehive. From that point until he reached the Sarsfield Bridge, he made good time; it was a little before three-thirty, so he had made that part of the trip more than a half-hour under his estimate. But now his troubles were about to begin. Not only did traffic suddenly become unmanageable, but a little red light began to glow on the dash. It pictured a battery, but Rollie had no idea what it meant. It was a new car with only 1500 miles registered on the odometer, so he believed that, whatever it was, it surely was minor. As soon as he was able, he turned into a service station. Fortunately, there were some mechanics on duty, or otherwise he might have been out of luck until Saturday.

"It's the fan belt," said the young man who had looked under the hood.

."How can that be?" Rollie answered. "This is a practically new car."

"Oh, it happens," the mechanic said. And it was fortunate for Rollie again, because if the station had not had the belt he needed (and he did get the last one), he probably would have had to wait until Saturday morning, since the supply center was out on O'Connell Street, ten full blocks from the station and directly along the route of all the afternoon traffic. It was fortunate, too, that he stopped when he did. The radiator most likely would have sprung a leak, and that would have caused considerable delay. As it was, Rollie judged that now he could never reach Tralee by six o'clock, to say nothing about being at Connor Pass by that time. Once again, his plans had taken an unexpected turn, so he decided to look for lodgings in Limerick once repairs were made. He paid the three pounds fifty for the fan belt and got a receipt. He knew the car agency would refund his money as long as he had the receipt. (On the '74 trip, they would have taken his word for any additional expense, even without the receipt. Rollie would not take that chance this time.)

The traffic was still very heavy, so Rollie decided to head toward Shannon, away from the flow of traffic. He had seen several B and B's and hotels along the way and counted upon a vacancy for the night. Within three blocks, he found a motor lodge, so he pulled into the parking lot. There was a vacancy, and although he assumed the room would be fairly noisy, situated as it was so near the highway, he thought it best to take it and not chance losing it while looking for a better place. Already today he had had too many close calls.

The room was clean and comfortable. As was so often the case, the toilet was shared by several rooms, but Rollie had become accustomed to this fact. He was, however, annoyed when he read the small sign above the sink in his room:

Do not use hot water in excess.
Heat for the night is 50p.

It was a hand-printed sign, a bit of local color. Four pounds fifty was a lot of money for the room, he thought, and he refused to pay anything additional. He banked on the hope that tonight would not be any chillier than last night in Galway; he hadn't needed additional warmth then. It was still warm outside, so he didn't think any more about it.

Rollie was in pretty good spirits despite the misadventures of the day. He had eaten a large breakfast, much larger than he normally did—even on vacation—but by now he was feeling hungry. He wasn't too far from downtown, so he decided to walk to the bridge, assuming that travelers on foot did not encounter the traffic problems of the drivers. He was correct in that assumption, and within twenty minutes was at the Hotel Royal George on Patrick Street, an extension of O'Connell. When he entered the hotel, he expected to see a sign to indicate the dining room and bar, but none was apparent. He looked through a few doors, but that didn't help. He did not like asking other guests for directions; it made him feel useless. He tried to look casual, as though he knew well what he was doing. He pretended he was deep in thought; he looked at his watch. All of this time, however, he carefully watched the people as they passed, waiting for a clue that would lead him to the bar. It would have been so simple to have asked the desk clerk, but Rollie was playing detective and was enjoying it; he was in no hurry. Before long, he overheard two men talking about getting a drink, so he followed them through a swinging door into the bar. It was situated right where he had thought it was, but he had not had the nerve to open the door himself unless he was positive. Rollie never wanted to be embarrassed by walking into a private party, thinking it was open to the public. He would rather take his time and be certain.

Rollie walked to the bar and ordered a lager. He sat beside two men who were talking about where they were going to dinner. It wasn't long before he was in conversation with them.

"Patrick Mulvany," he said, "and I'm pleased to meet you, Rollie. Staying long in Limerick, are you?"

"No. Just tonight," Rollie said. "Can I buy you a drink?"

"Thank you. A lager for me," said Michael O'Brien, the other man who lived in Limerick. "I think Pat's is the same."

"You say that Galway is always this busy during the races?" Rollie asked.

"Indeed it is," answered Pat. "Why Dublin is no busier during the horse show."

"And why do you Irishmen get such pleasure taking your vacation so close to home? I would think that you'd travel to the Continent for a week or so," said Rollie.

"And don't you think we like our own country?" Mike answered. "Sure, the drink is as good in Galway as it is in London!"

"And you don't always come to Ireland, now do you?" said Pat, forcing Rollie to smile and think about what he had just asked.

"I guess not," Rollie said, "but there's a lot more territory in America than in Ireland, and each place is so different."

"And do you think we're all alike, then?" said Mike.

All three were smiling by now, and Rollie realized they were baiting him and enjoying it. Through the conversation, Rollie learned that Mike was a factory worker from just outside Dublin. He and a few friends had spent the first four days of the week in Galway at the races, and he described it as a continuous drunken party. He thought that he had spent 400 pounds, but was not sure. He was single, had a small sports car, and spent every penny he earned. He loved the life he was living. Rollie thought that a foolish way to spend his money and told him so. He also thought Mike was a liar, especially about having spent 400 pounds in less than a week. Pat, a salesman who operated a business nearby, had stopped in Limerick to visit Mike for a bit.

Rollie talked with them for about an hour, each buying the other a drink as the occasion demanded. By around six-thirty, Mike and Pat left, and Rollie was left sitting alone at the bar.

The room was by no means empty, but little groups had formed at the numerous tables and Rollie was not part of any of them. The bar in front of him was covered with thirty or forty dirty glasses, and the bartender, a girl who looked to be about eighteen, made no attempt to wash them and put them away. Rollie decided it was time to leave, so he downed the last bit of beer in his glass and headed out the door.

Rollie looked up and down the street and decided to walk toward the intersection and cross to O'Connell, where he could see several restaurants. Tonight he decided to have an American meal, to leave the sandwiches and scones for another time. (The thought did cross his mind that sandwiches and scones were typically tourist and not Irish.) He longed for a good steak, and he hoped the restaurant into which he turned could satisfy this wish. There was only a very short wait before a hostess showed him to a table. He sat down next to a very young couple, who, he discovered after a few minutes, were on their honeymoon. They were Americans from New York City, and one of the couple had relatives in Ireland. Rollie didn't want to intrude upon them, so he limited his conversation to these few questions and said no more.

The menu did list a steak, so Rollie ordered it. He was thinking about a thick New York sirloin, and when the waitress arrived with the small, three-quarter–inch, well-done piece of meat, he was disappointed. "They don't cook their steaks any better than they make their martinis," he muttered, loud enough so the waitress asked if he wanted something, but soft enough so she could not hear what he had said.

"Thank you, no," he said. "This is just fine," and she left him to enjoy his dinner. Actually, the steak, although overdone for his taste, was very good. The two choices of potatoes were acceptable, and the vegetable seasoned pleasantly. The meal was unusually good, and, as far as Rollie could remember, one of the best he had had on this trip. Perhaps he had tried too many of the smaller town restaurants to draw an accurate conclusion about Irish restaurants, but aside from the meal he had had at Snaffles, this one was the best on this trip. He lingered awhile over some Irish Mist, which he had decided upon rather than a dessert or Irish coffee. As he was sipping his drink, he noticed a woman across from him who looked remarkably like his own Barbara. It was not until this very moment that he had thought about his wife. Now he remembered that he had not sent a card when he should have. Most likely, even if he were to send one tomorrow, it would not arrive until after he had returned home, and then what good would that have done? He dismissed the thought of Barbara as quickly as it had come; he was on vacation, and he refused to think about home. But he did think about Anna and about what might happen on Wednesday when he returned to Dublin. He believed he would not again allow himself to become depressed over people, even Anna.

While Rollie was lost in thought, the waitress had asked twice if he would care for anything else, and it was only after the second question that he became aware of her standing next to him.

"Thank you, but no. Everything was fine. My check, please," and she left him for the moment. Rollie finished his drink, collected the check on his way to the cashier, paid his bill, and left.

Rollie was startled a bit as he entered the street. It was raining and had grown much cooler during the hour and a half he had been in the restaurant. He pulled the collar of his coat around his neck and overlapped the lapels, but he still could feel the cold. He realized that he had a thirty minute walk to his room, and he did not look forward to arriving there wet and cold. He looked for a taxi, but none was available. He turned and headed for the bridge; he had no alternative but to walk.

As Rollie opened the door to his room, he regretted not having paid the extra fifty pence for heat. But as soon as he shed the wet clothes, dried himself, and slipped between the covers, he forgot all about the cold and rain. Tomorrow would be fine, he thought. A good, early night's sleep would get him on the road before dawn. Time was now becoming short, and he had too much to see to allow anything else to get in the way. He no more than began to think about the events of the past day when he fell sound asleep.

When Rollie arose on Saturday morning, it was still dark. He fumbled some for his shoes and socks, put them on, and sat on the edge of his bed, scratching his head. The night's sleep had been refreshing, and he looked forward to his journey through Adare—where he might stop to go through the Prince's Palace—and on to Tralee and the mountains of Connor Pass. This morning, he did not think about breakfast; he thought only about the drive and the pleasure that was waiting for him. He dressed, gathered his things, checked to be certain that nothing would be left behind, and headed for the car. He had taken only his small bag to the room, since he had no intention of staying in Limerick beyond this one night. It was chilly this morning, but the rain had stopped. He carefully placed his bag in the backseat of the car and climbed into the driver's seat. He turned the key in the ignition, and the motor turned over but did not catch. Thinking that he had flooded it, Rollie waited several minutes before trying a second time. Nothing. He then placed his foot firmly on the accelerator pedal, held it to the floor, and turned the key. As before, the motor turned over but did not catch. Rollie thought for a moment and decided the plugs and points were probably still damp from the night before and needed a little more time to dry. It was beginning to get light out, and he could see people stirring in the houses nearby. *Perhaps breakfast is the answer,* he thought, and he got out of the car and went back inside the hotel. It would be but three-quarters of an hour until breakfast. He could wait.

CHAPTER EIGHT

On Friday morning, the McCormick household did not stir until after ten o'clock. The children were all late sleepers, especially when summer jobs were not an issue, and the adults had been up late partying. Barbara was first to rise, and she put on a full pot of coffee. She knew well that she and Polly would sit for an hour or longer talking about all that had happened, not only last night, but since the two had last been together. On Thursday, Barbara had arrived only an hour or so before the party, and although she was able to lend a hand with the preparations, she did not get any opportunity to talk with Polly. This morning, the children would be in and out very quickly; none of them could stand sitting around the house. Chris, Polly's oldest, had planned to conduct a tour of the new plaza, and all three of Barbara's children agreed to go with her. Afterwards, they all planned to try roller-skating at the new rink just opposite the plaza. Mike would take his coffee and go out to the garage. He had a project to finish and spent much of his spare time attending to that matter. He wouldn't tell Polly what it was, so she assumed it was a present, perhaps a table or chair, since Mike often spent time refinishing furniture and sometimes building new pieces. After brief scurrying around the kitchen, there would be time for a long talk.

Barbara, often casual about her appearance, had just thrown a robe over her shoulders when she went to make the coffee. Beneath the robe she wore a short nightgown that Rollie had given to her on her last birthday. She liked the short nightgown, especially on hot summer nights, because it covered her sufficiently and yet allowed her free movement in bed. It was a comfortable piece of clothing in which to sleep. When she went to answer the door, she had forgotten that she had not yet gotten dressed.

"Just get up?" came Hobie's first remark. It was obvious that Barbara had been in bed only a short time ago.

"Oh, Hobie. What brings you here this morning? It is morning, isn't it?" Barbara asked. She politely opened the door while at the same time she pulled the robe together and tied it. It was very plain that she had not intended to flirt with Hobie. The initial picture of Barbara standing there, with her long, slender legs and beautiful blonde hair falling gently to her shoulders, was difficult for Hobie to dismiss.

"Where is everyone? The party too much?" Hobie asked.

"Everyone's just now getting up," Barbara answered. "I guess there was no reason to rush it." She closed the door, and Hobie followed her to the kitchen.

"Would you like a cup?" she asked.

"Thanks. I would," Hobie answered. "You people got any plans for today?"

"I think Mike and Polly were going to take a ride to Minnesota this afternoon to show me the property they're thinking about buying," said Barbara, "but I'm sure we've not thought at all about tonight."

"Why don't you all come over to my place for a cookout?" Hobie seemed most emphatic. "Janice felt a lot better this morning and thought she should make amends for last night."

"Janice doesn't have anything to apologize for," said Barbara. "If you can't get feeling good at a party, then I guess you shouldn't have parties!" Barbara was alluding to the conversation with Karl and the others on the topic of the upcoming election.

"Mike, you son of a gun, how do you feel this morning?" Hobie called out. He saw Mike pass the hall door as he descended the stairs.

"I thought everyone had gone home," Mike said with a smile. "How'd we miss you?"

"You know me; once a party starts, I'm good until all the booze is gone. I still see a few full bottles on the counter." It was an illusion of Hobie's that he was the first to get to a party and the last to leave. Except for the first meeting of the Fish Talers when Hobie and Janice stayed until after 3:00 A.M. only because Hobie had fallen asleep on the couch and missed the swim Janice and the others had taken in the pond around two in the morning, Hobie always wanted to leave a party early. Rarely did he and Janice stay beyond midnight, and then only when an early-morning breakfast was prepared. But Hobie insisted he was one among the great party men.

"Any coffee, Barbara?" Mike asked. "I could use a cup." Mike made his way into the kitchen and grabbed a cup. "Polly is in the bathroom; she'll be down in a minute."

"A minute, nothing!" Polly said as she walked into the kitchen. "I've been up for hours." She was fibbing, of course.

"What are you doing here, Hobie? I thought we sent you home early last night." Polly grinned at him.

"I don't know why you're all on me this morning," Hobie countered. "Isn't a guy welcome anymore?" And the inane chatter went on goodnaturedly for another few minutes.

Barbara could see that she would not have an opportunity to talk with Polly as she planned, so she excused herself and went into her bedroom to change, leaving Polly and Hobie to talk about arrangements for the evening. The room in which she had slept was the remodeled closet, and although it had been nearly completed, a few items still needed finishing. For example, the door handle had not yet been affixed, so when Barbara swung the door closed after her, it did not stay fast, but sprang slightly open. When Mike closed the kitchen door to head toward the workship, the breeze pushed Barbara's door further open, leaving Hobie a full view of Barbara in the bedroom.

Barbara stood naked, her back to Hobie, limply clutching the light nightgown she had been wearing. She stared at her suitcase as though wondering what she should choose to wear this morning. As she turned to place the nightwear on the bed, she noticed Hobie looking at her and, without hesitation or the least embarrassment, calmly pushed the door closed and moved behind it.

Hobie nearly spilled his cup of coffee as he awkwardly placed it on the table. He found it impossible to keep from staring at Barbara, and as she turned toward him it completed his picture of that lovely vision, a slim, firm body with a stomach slightly protruding, serving only to accent the beauty he observed. Hobie broke into a cold sweat and heard nothing of what Polly had been saying for the past thirty seconds.

"We'll be back around six, Hobie. Hobie?" Polly raised her voice. She was unaware of Hobie's preoccupation.

"Six?" said Hobie, not sure what she meant.

"From Minnesota," Polly explained.

"Oh, yes, that'll be fine. I'll tell Janice to break out the good booze for tonight," he said, trying to make light of his inability to discern—immediately—what Polly was talking about. "We'll probably have hamburgers, if that's all right with everyone," and he glanced toward the bedroom door.

"I'm sure that after last night, hamburgers will be welcome. Can't live too long on all that rich stuff," Polly said, confident now that Hobie understood what they were talking about.

Barbara came back into the kitchen looking cheerful as ever and sat down next to Hobie with a second cup of coffee, which she had filled as she passsed the counter.

"Did you get things fixed for tonight?" she asked Hobie, as though nothing much had happened during the last ten minutes except the conversation between Hobie and Polly.

"Once I got his attention," Polly said, "we were able to plan a bit. What were you thinking about, anyway?" Polly asked.

Hobie reddened visibly, but replied, "Oh, some deep, philosophical question like what I was supposed to get at the grocery store for Janice. Actually, that's the reason I'm out so early this morning," he said, trying to make light of the whole thing. Barbara never gave any indication to either of them that she was aware of what Hobie had seen. As a matter of fact, she was so calm and undisturbed by the event that Hobie seriously questioned whether or not Barbara really did know what he had seen and for how long.

"How about cocktails at six and cookout whenever anyone gets hungry?" he asked. "And bring the kids; I think they'll enjoy being a part of it for once." He had to force his last comment, since he would rather that Barbara came by herself.

"Sounds pretty good to me," said Aliceanne, who had been standing by the corner eating an orange. "What do you think, Jerry?" she asked her brother.

"It's time they started treating us as adults," he responded, half joking and half serious. "We can't keep skating and visiting plazas every time we come to visit," he added, trying to make his point without belittling Joan, indirectly, for the plans she had made. He added, "Joan must get tired of providing for the relatives from the East," and he felt he had gotten out of that situation well.

"I'm willing to do anything, as long as it's not work; I'm on vacation," and with that comment Barbara got up and put a piece of bread in the toaster.

"Well, I better be on my way; Janice is going to wonder what happened to me," and the statement was more ironic than he knew. "See you tonight," Hobie called as he went out the front door. About twenty minutes later, Barbara and the McCormicks piled into the station wagon and headed for the north and the new property.

☆ ☆ ☆

Friday afternoons in Decorah were always fairly busy, and this Friday was no exception. Hobie did not live far from Mike and Polly, but it took about three times longer to get there tonight. Barbara had always talked about the "Friday night farmers" and how they filed into downtown to see what was happening—and when Barbara and the others all started on the way to the Hofstaders, downtown was already bustling with the crowd. If everyone had a particular destination, the traffic would probably have moved along well, but so many really had no idea where they were headed and drove exceedingly slow, trying to decide. The Friday night crowd always upset Mike, and he usually never left home on a Friday until well after seven o'clock, when the roads were again clear. Tonight they left well before seven, for they arrived at the Hofstaders just a few minutes after six.

"Welcome to Paradise," called Janice from the redwood deck. "We've been expecting you," she added, changing her voice in an attempt to imitate a notorious villain.

"And how are you feeling tonight?" came Polly's voice from the open window at the back of the wagon.

"Just great," Janice answered. "I must have got the wrong mixtures last night," she said, smiling and waving her hands to indicate that she had been unsteady. "It's amazing what a good night's sleep can do," and she came down from the deck to greet her guests. "This is what I like so much about summer, one party after another."

"Did you get that chair finished?" Hobie shouted to Mike. Hobie had been in the garage getting some charcoal for the grill.

"It's coming along," Mike answered, "but all of these eating and drinking events are seriously affecting my progress." Mike liked to party as much as anyone else and had no particular schedule for finishing any of the variety of items on which he was working. It was a hobby; when things got finished or whether they got finished did not disturb him in the least. Nor did it bother Polly. She had added a few beautiful pieces of furniture to the house from Mike's work, but she took that to be a bonus.

"Don't kid yourself," said Polly, directing her remarks to Hobie. "Mike has never passed up an opportunity to eat yet, so he isn't likely to let an old chair stand in his way!" They all laughed at that.

While all of this talking was going on, Barbara had gotten out of the car and walked to the garden. The Hofstaders had a large flower garden, which extended from the edge of the driveway to the property line at the back of the lot, an area that comprised about one-fifth of an acre. Part of the garden was developed within the wooded area that circled the whole housing development and was replete with all kinds of green herbs and flowers. The section that was close to the house had a variety of bright flowers, mostly annuals, which attracted the eye as soon as one came down the driveway. The garden demanded a great deal of attention, and that job fell to Janice. She loved working in the garden and took great pride in all that she had accomplished with it.

"You've expanded the garden quite a bit since I last saw it, haven't you?" asked Barbara as she moved through the paths leading to the several sections. "I don't remember this section in the woods," she said, turning to greet Janice, who had followed her into the garden.

"I guess you're right," Janice answered. "To me, it seems like it has always been there." And they both moved slowly, viewing each variety and making comments as they went.

Hobie had not taken his eyes off Barbara from the time she had gotten out of the car . He tried to busy himself with details about the grill, but if anyone had paid serious attention to what he was doing, it would have been obvious that the picking up and putting down of charcoal and grill made little sense. He made no effort to try to blank out that picture of her standing in the bedroom. During these first few minutes, that image grew more vivid than ever. Hobie was beginning to feel as if he had fallen in love again.

The children had picked up a football and were throwing it around the yard. There was enough room to have a little game of touch, so Jerry made the suggestion. Mike joined the five children, and for about twenty minutes they played, three on a side. It was fairly warm, so by the time they had finished the game, everyone was thirsty. The kids got into the pop—even Barbara's children, none of whom drank beer or liquor, despite the fact that in New York they were old enough to drink—and Mike made himself a large martini; what else!

By seven-thirty, the coals were perfect and everyone was ready to eat. Hobie cooked up a batch of hot dogs and hamburgers and served them to the children first. Once the five of them were fed, he concentrated on the others. By eight o'clock, everyone had been served, so he could relax and enjoy the food and drink. Hobie sat next to Mike and chatted about the possibility of fishing later in September. Mike had often fished much later in the season than the others, and Hobie had thought that he might enjoy it, too. The fanfare and commotion of opening day would certainly not be present, but the other enjoyable aspects of camping would be. In addition, the weather would not be nearly so severe as it often was on opening day, and that fact, in itself, tempted one to "try it out," as Mike often had said when he tried to coax his friends to go along on these late-season trips. Tonight, Hobie was on the verge of making a commitment for a weekend in the near future.

Barbara and Janice were sitting across from the men and had renewed the conversation that they had been having in the garden. Barbara would like to have had a large garden at the lake—there certainly was enough room—and she felt that Janice could offer some constructive advice about how she might develop one. It was interesting to know that Barbara had never before thought to consult Janice about gardens, despite the fact that Janice had been a gardener for years and always had many varieties of flowers in bloom around the house throughout the summer months. This thought occurred to Barbara as she sat talking with Janice, and she reasoned that asking Janice's advice probably came from the fact that she was so impressed with the effect created in the new wooded section of the Hofstader garden. The conversation was greatly to Barbara's liking, since it never deteriorated, as she would put it, to the level of babies and toilet training. Polly, too, managed easily to indulge in this kind of talk, and although she did not care to keep a flower garden, she enjoyed this one and at her own house did keep a lovely backyard, especially the area that surrounded the pond. There was a mutual respect that existed between Polly and Janice, each enjoying the other's yard accomplishments, as it were.

By nine o'clock, as darkness was beginning to descend, the conversation began to wane, and Janice started to carry dishes and silverware to the kitchen. Polly helped, and Barbara said she wanted to take one more look at the wooded area. Barbara still had a partially filled drink, so she took it with her. Hobie, still keeping an eye on Barbara, caught up to her just as she reached the section of the garden farthest from the house.

"I think Janice has done a great job out here," Hobie volunteered as he approached Barbara.

"Oh, it's beautiful," Barbara responded. "It's so clever how she has used the natural paths and built the garden to conform to that design. I don't think it could have been planned any better," and she continued to walk around some of the more intricate rock designs that marked the juncture of several different shrubs that also had a prominent place in the garden.

"It's not too warm tonight, is it?" asked Hobie as he searched for something to say that would seem natural and casual.

"No, it's not," said Barbara, paying little attention to Hobie or to what he was saying.

Hobie thought of the morning and began to experience a similar sensation to that which he had felt at the kitchen table. He moved close to Barbara, took her in his arms, and kissed her, hoping that she would understand, and more, that she would share his feelings.

Barbara held her drink between them, offering no resistance to Hobie's embrace. When Hobie finally released her, he was trembling with excitement. Barbara had no romantic feelings for Hobie; she had always thought of him as a friend, and that was all. She did not share this infatuation that he felt and demonstrated, and she was puzzled by his advances. She never once thought about Thursday night when she had asked him to hold her, and, in fact, she might well have asked the same of anyone who had been standing there by the pond with her.

Hobie started to speak and at the same time took a step toward Barbara, as though to repeat what he had done just seconds before. Barbara lifted her hand and softly asked him to stop, saying only, "Hobie, it's time we went back to the house." She turned and headed for the deck leaving Hobie standing there, speechless. He was crestfallen, especially since he now realized what a foolish thing he had done. He would have been even more upset if he had known that Janice, who had returned to the deck to remind Hobie to bring the card table from the garage, had seen everything that had happened.

CHAPTER NINE

Rollie's trip to Connor Pass on Saturday morning was delayed only until ten o'clock, when the mechanic got to work. He discovered that indeed it was the points, already worn and needing replacement. This fact puzzled Rollie even more than the broken fan belt, but he didn't question it this time. He wanted to get going, so he thanked the mechanic for coming immediately to the hotel, for discovering the problem so quickly, and for making short work of it. By 10:45, Rollie was on his way.

The going through Limerick this Saturday morning was smooth, with little traffic, which moved along well. Rollie headed southwest on N21 and figured he would be in Tralee no later than two o'clock. The sun had come out strong, and the day was beautiful. It was considerably warmer now than it had been last night. Rollie noticed that as he got farther and farther south, the rocks disappeared and more and more lush pasture came into view. Rollie did not want to chance missing the Connor Pass today, so when he arrived in Adare he drove through, not even stopping for anything to eat. Eating could be done in Tralee, if he, in fact, ate at all that afternoon.

For the next hour, Rollie drove at a steady rate, stopping very seldom at intersections through the small villages along the way. Only once did he really lose any time, and that was just south of Abbeyfeale, where he got behind a farmer who was driving his sheep along the road, probably moving from one pasture to another. There wasn't room for the car to pass, so he simply stayed behind the sheep until, at last, the farmer saw fit to move them off the thoroughfare. By 2:15, Rollie was in Tralee and at the base of the mountains that he must climb, both to once again see the view from the pass and to get to Dingle, his ultimate objective for the day.

The climb was slow, not so much because of traffic or obstacles in his path, but because the road was exceedingly narrow and winding. Often he could not see more than 100 yards ahead and was never quite certain about the room he would have on the turns or the kind of traffic approaching in the opposite direction. Other cars did not present much of a problem, but buses were a real hazard. Although he had not encountered any buses yet today, he did remember one occasion on the '74 trip when he was traveling west of Galway and on a sudden turn was forced off the road by a tourist bus, which didn't appear to slow down, even for tight turns. (He cursed the Irish bus driver that day!)

It took Rollie little more than twenty minutes to reach the summit, and once he arrived, he headed for the parking lot he remembered was situated overlooking the southwestern view. The lot was there and empty, so he was able to park directly in view of the area below. Very near the car were a number of grazing sheep, the backs of which were marked with bright blue. Rollie had learned that the colors identified the owners, and consequently one would discover many different colored sheep throughout this area. It was strange: no farmhouse could be seen anywhere around, but it was obvious that these sheep were not wild. Rollie had also learned that the Irish were most trusting and assumed that only the owner of the sheep would have any reason to watch after them or take them. On one occasion, Rollie had noticed piles of turf along the road and, knowing how farmers needed this fuel, inquired whether it was safe, unguarded as it was, since anyone might come along and take it. He was told that no one except the owner would touch it. "And why not?" Rollie asked.

"Because it wouldn't be his," came the reply. Rollie questioned no further.

Rollie looked out over the countryside. He could see small thatch-roofed houses in the distance; he saw streams, hills, and miles and miles of pasture, green and brown, and large areas covered with those wild yellow flowers, the name of which he did not learn. It was a beautiful sight, and he swelled with such a wonderful feeling that tears came to his eyes. He wondered how many visitors—and even those native Irishmen from farther away—had ever experienced the emotional exhilaration this scene provided. Of course, the farmers here saw it daily, but he wondered if even they appreciated its splendor. Then a strange thing happened. As he closed his eyes to breathe deeply and prepare to take in the view once more, drops of rain began wetting his face. He opened his eyes and, in disbelief, could see nothing below through the downpour. Within minutes, the sun returned and the beauty was restored. *How could it be,* he thought, *that at one minute there was not a cloud in the sky and at the next clouds were so dense that almost nothing was visible?* And no matter how long he waited at this spot on top of the mountain, this marvel repeated itself. And the sheep kept on grazing as if nothing extraordinary had occurred.

Rollie spent more than an hour on top of the mountain, and the longer he stayed, the more he saw. At one point, his vision seemed so unobstructed that the details of the surrounding countryside could be seen for miles; he could never remember, in all his forty years in America, ever having seen air so pure and uncluttered by the byproducts of industry. But he could not allow himself this pleasure any longer, and he began his descent to the lowlands on the other side of the mountain. Connor Pass would come soon, and he must save ample time for that sight as well.

Like so much of what Rollie had enjoyed on this second visit to his father's native land, the pass provided its share of beauty. The area around the pass was not land on which one might build or farm, but seemed made for the sole purpose of providing the Irish with a national monument. The rock formations were varied, as though a miniature Grand Canyon, vestiges of an ice-age past. Rollie needed to pay attention to his driving, however, for the road was narrow and the lower level a long way down. It was difficult for a single person to both drive the pass and observe the beauty it presented. There were very few places for a car to pull safely off the road, and even in those areas designed for that purpose, very little room was left for other cars to pass. It was as though the viewer was allowed only a glimpse of the beauty, his ration as it were, and then commanded to drive on. But for Rollie, such thoughts made him smile, knowing that however little he may see of all of this, it was more than most people would see in a lifetime. How lucky he was to have discovered this "island of the beauty of God." And, deep in thought, he sideswiped a bus that was ascending the hill, and that brought him out of his trance and back to reality. He had barely touched the bus, so there was no need to stop and survey the damage. This was very fortunate for both parties for had there been need to assess the damage to the vehicles, both would probably have been unable to stop until several miles apart. Rollie would pay more attention to his driving from now on.

By the time Rollie had completed his drive through Connor Pass, it was about six o'clock, and he was no more than a mile from Dingle. He had heard about a delightful country home in Baile na nGall, a Mrs. Nic Gearailt's, so he looked for a public telephone as he arrived. He had no difficulty locating one on the main street, and he placed a call to the proprietress. (His pronounciation of her name was not good, but he managed.)

"Hello," came the voice on the other end.

"Hello," said Rollie. "I am looking for a room for tonight. Would you have one available?" Rollie had been cautioned about calling, since this home was one very popular with the Irish; it was so remote that few visitors would ever find it, except by accident.

"Well, I do," she said, "and would you be arrivin' soon?" she continued in a matter-of-fact tone.

"As soon as I can find you," Rollie answered, informing her of his whereabouts, pleased that he had a place to stay so near the coastline.

"Well, then, Mr. Welch, I'll be expectin' you," and she had no difficulty pronouncing his name!

"Thank you very much," said Rollie. "I look forward to the evening," and he hoped he had made himself clear. He replaced the receiver and returned to the car. Now to find Bally na gall, as he pronounced it. Finding the home was not an easy matter, despite the directions he had received from the owner of the restaurant where he had stopped about an hour later. Rollie had followed the map exactly, and although he could not always find street signs at every road, he was fairly certain that his destination could not be too distant.

"Go out the door, turn right, and go straight to Mrs. Gearailt. Yes, this is Baile na nGall, and she's five minutes down the road," said the gentleman. Rollie thanked him and finished his sandwich and sweet. The Irish seemed insulted if you neglected to have a sweet with your meal.

"Remember," called the gentleman as Rollie prepared to leave, "go neither left nor right, but straight to Mrs. Nic Gearailt," and Rollie waved a polite thanks as he drove off.

No more than five minutes later, and probably less than that, Rollie came to a T in the road. "Go neithr left nor right," echoed in his mind, and he stopped the car. There was no Mrs. Nic Gearailt's in sight, just a bar on the left and several rundown houses directly in his path. He turned into theparking lot and went into the bar.

"Mrs. Nic Gearailt is just down the road," came the answer to his question, so he left the bar and continued to the left, hopeful that the house would be nearby. He remembered that the man in the restaurant had told him that the church would be on the corner, just across from the house, so Rollie thought it should be easy enough to spot. He had driven for half an hour, seemingly in circles, when he finally spotted the church. Right across from the church was a beautiful, new house and a sign at the entrance to the rocky driveway that announced Mrs. Nic Gearailt's. He had arrived at last.

Later that evening, when he had time to think about what had happened in that forty-five minutes or so when he was searching for the home that was "no more than five minutes down the road," he realized what had happened. The home was that close to the restaurant, but one had to bend around a few houses—to the right, as one approached the turning in the road. The precision of the directions given him had the effect of a mother telling her child to "come straight home from school," which meant not so much "straight" as it meant "directly" and could involve a few turns. Well, it was a lesson learned and one not to forget, especially in Ireland.

Rollie's room was very comfortable, with two large double beds, two sinks, a shower, and a large picture window looking out on the yard at the rear of the home, providing a perfect view of the mountains in the distance. What luxury for such an out-of-the-way guest home. There wasn't a store for miles, but the accommodations here were excellent. Rollie thought the house was no more than a year old, judging by the unfinished driveway and back porch. He admired the woodwork in the room, very rich-looking mahogany paneling throughout. There was no mistake, however: the shower door was also of this rich wood, and already the door was warping from the humidity. Even the window side of the drapes had deposits of mildew, and Rollie thought it would be less than a year before new doors and drapes would be needed. It was unfortunate that the mistake could not have been avoided, for it appeared that the owner had made attempts to provide an attractive and quality guest house. It was a bargain at four pounds a day, breakfast included.

Rollie showered and changed into fresh clothes. It was still fairly early, and he did not want to retire just yet. He put on his pajamas, crawled between the covers, and opened a new volume of Macken: *I Am Alone*. This was the only volume of Macken that Rollie had not yet read. He looked forward to an enjoyable few hours, reading again about the adopted country he was fast becoming a part of. It was very quiet here, with no traffic noise and none of the bustle of the city. Rollie could understand why the native city dwellers might take a holiday here in their own country.

Rollie read for just a few minutes and looked up from his book. He felt uncomfortable and hungry; the lunch he had had a few hours ago was not sufficient, he thought, to get him through the night. Besides, he was a bit chilly. It had become colder the last hour, and the heat had not yet been turned on in his room. He got up, put on his trousers over his pajamas, dressed in the shirt he had worn that afternoon, put on his shoes and socks, and went out into the hallway. He knocked on what he supposed was Mrs. Nic Gearailt's door and asked the woman who answered if it would be possible to get a pot of tea.

"Would you be wantin' supper, then?" she asked.

"No thank you, just a pot of tea." And Rollie would have been most appreciative of the tea.

"Well, go into the sitting room and I'll bring it there," she said, and Rollie turned and headed into the room at the end of the hall. He was surprised to find several other guests sitting there, some talking by the fire, others watching the television. He nodded to all as he entered, and sat in a comfortable rocker on one side of the fire. Within five minutes, a young girl brought tea, along with several pieces of buttered brown bread.

"Thank you very much," Rollie said.

"You're welcome," she replied and turned and walked out of the room.

Rollie felt warm, both inside and out, as he drank the tea and sat by the fire. It was not long before he was talking to a gentleman sitting next to him smoking a pipe. He was a Mr. O'Doyle, from Kilkenny, taking a few days of leisure.

"Have you come here before?" Rollie asked, wondering if he had found someone who could verify the stories he had heard about Mrs. Nic Gearailt's home.

"For the past three years," Mr. O'Doyle answered, indicating that the home had been built three years ago and only recently had the showers begun working. This information, of course, showed Rollie that he had been mistaken about his initial assessment concerning when the home was built, but very accurate about the time when doors and drapes would need to be replaced.

"Why do you come out here?" Rollie asked.

"Well, now, you're here, aren't you," O'Doyle responded without appearing to be asking a question.

"I mean, it wouldn't seem like much of a vacation to me if I couldn't spend some time in a place that isn't like the town where I spend most of the time during the year," Rollie said. He was trying to make a point, but the Irishman would not cooperate.

"And I wonder why anyone would come to Ireland while

we are trying to get out," O'Doyle said.

"A good point," answered Rollie and changed the subject. "Is that your car in the driveway?" Rollie asked.

"It is," answered O'Doyle. It was so difficult to get an Irishman to give you more than that for which you'd asked.

"How's the mileage?" Rollie asked.

"Good," he said and added, "A lot better than those big American cars."

"Are you concerned about the gas shortage?" and Rollie immediately recognized his error in calling petrol gas. But O'Doyle did not embarrass him—this time.

"I am, but this one's got a converter. I left it in the shop before I took holidays and had the mechanic make a bottle gas switchover," he said.

"You mean that your car can run on liquid gas?" Rollie asked in amazement.

"We've been doing it for a few years," O'Doyle responded. Rollie wondered if Americans had yet thought of that.

"Does that give you good mileage?" Rollie asked, believing that he had discovered some "hot" information to take back home.

"Not in the least," said O'Doyle, "but there's ample supply and it's cheap." He indicated that the cost did not exceed what he would spend on petrol and sometimes it was a bit less expensive. "There's one problem," said O'Doyle, offering some advice that had not been asked for. "If the conversion work is not done properly, the car is liable to explode." That information ended any plans Rollie may have had to experiment with a change in his car back home.

Rollie finished his tea and bread and could feel sleep approaching. He had enjoyed his talk with O'Doyle, but now he wanted to be alone. He got up, shook O'Doyle's hand, said that he hoped to see him soon, and went back to his room.

Once in his room, Rollie opened Macken again and started to read. It was now dark outside, and he could see lights flickering in the distance. The window had fogged, and he judged it was becoming colder. The book was as interesting as the others, but he could not concentrate on it. After several attempts to get through the first few pages, he closed the book, turned off the light, and snuggled under the covers. It had been another good day; he had seen all that he had planned for Saturday. Tomorrow he would leave for Bantry Bay. It was one place he had missed in '74, and he had regretted that fact. Bantry was a coastal city, tucked back into the land, having the advantages of the sea and the protection of the land. He knew it was a small town, and he hoped he would get more of the feeling of what being on the coast was like than he had found during his stay in Galway. And he thought, too, that he would be a day nearer Dublin. That night he dreamed of Anna.

CHAPTER TEN

The little incident with Hobie on Friday night upset Barbara. She did not like to think that a married woman had always to be on her guard against men, especially when those men were supposed to be close friends. She knew she was living in the twentieth century, with the vanishing of the sanctity of marriage, the lowering of moral standards, and other such things, but she had always thought that those stories were describing other people. She had heard about parties where married couples exchanged house keys and couples paired up with friends to spend a night in a strange bed, but she always thought that more fiction than reality. Never in her life had she ever given any thought at all to the possibility that she could be the object of the affections of a man other than her husband. She was not a prude, but she did retain respect for the institution of marriage. She could accept divorce due to the incompatibility of the parties concerned, but she judged men scoundrels (and women as well) who would seek divorce because of their own infidelity. This was so unacceptable to her; yet it could easily have happened had she been a willing party. The more she dwelled on the subject, the more disgusting it became to her. Yet she did not for a moment believe that what had happened with Hobie came anywhere near to all of these thoughts about marriage problems and lovers.

Barbara could not get to sleep on Friday night. It was difficult to stay much after ten o'clock at the Hofstaders, and she was very relieved when Janice did not insist that everyone play cards for a few hours, an activity that they all enjoyed and quite often would participate in for several hours after supper. Of course, Mike and Polly had no idea that Hobie had made advances toward Barbara, and Barbara was unaware that Janice knew about what had happened. The children, especially Polly's, were anxious to leave as well, so the party broke up around ten. When the Hofstaders were finally alone, Janice said little to Hobie except that she had seen him in the garden with Barbara and that she thought it cruel of him to have done what he did. Hobie had no answer, and by the time Janice had gone to bed, Hobie had made himself another drink and sat alone on the deck. Things in the Hofstader household would soon take a turn for the worse, but tonight all would remain status quo.

By six-thirty in the morning, Barbara gave up hope of getting to sleep and got up and went for a walk in the backyard. When she reached the pond, she sat down on the bank and watched the reflection of the trees in the water and the curious cloud formations as the sun made its way in the east. She began to think of Rollie and wished he were here. This would never have happened, she thought, had Rollie been on this trip. The men would have been together for the whole time, and the women would have had delightful talks about many things, each one as delighted to hear the other, as desirous of telling her own story. *That is the way it had always been and the way it should be,* she thought. She wondered if Rollie was thinking about her and thought how nice it would have been had she and Rollie taken the trip together, without the children. She frowned when she thought that such a possibility had been suggested by Rollie, but Barbara had felt her eagerness to go somewhere warmer would have been enough to dissuade Rollie from returning to Ireland. Yet she had been wrong and now felt an urgent need to be with her husband. She remembered her need to be held, but it was Rollie she wanted, not Hobie, and the love she felt for Rollie suddenly began to intensify, and she started to reminisce about Rollie and his work.

Barbara had forgotten how much she admired the work that Rollie had done at the academy. Rollie was a strong teacher, a leader, and it was difficult to mount opposition to the improvements he sought at school. She remembered the "skirmish" he had had with the principal over the way the school secretary typed tests. Rollie insisted the secretary follow the logical rules of test construction; the principal insisted the tests be typed most efficiently—to save paper. The principal won the first round, but Rollie every one after. The logic of his argument predominated, and future tests were prepared as Rollie had requested. Then there was the time when Bill McCarthy opposed the new syllabus that Rollie had restructured (and for which the school had paid him $400) and insisted that the current syllabus was good enough. (Bill had been a moderately effective department head for a number of years.) Rollie couldn't talk sense to Bill, but he did convince the rest of the staff that the new syllabus was by far superior to the old, and the school adopted the new one, despite Bill's protestations.

The one event that Barbara remembered most, however, was the situation in 1970 when the senior class revolted and decided to ignore the principal and do what was traditional. It seemed that after the annual senior banquet, several of the football players decided to celebrate at a lakeside bar and, after too many drinks, managed to destroy a shuffleboard and a plate-glass window in the bar. The next day, the owner of the bar called the school and demanded satisfaction for the damages. The owner did not know any of the boys by name, but he did know that all of those involved were seniors at the academy. The principal assured the owner that the matter would be handled to his satisfaction and called an assembly of the senior class that afternoon. The message at the assembly was simple: all members were guilty, damages must be paid, and the senior ball would be cancelled. The principal was taking a strong stand (the first stand of any kind he had ever taken!) and he indicated that such behavior on the part of the seniors was totally unacceptable.

The seniors, for the most part, were not rowdies, and they felt that those responsible should make restitution. However, they were unanimous in their feelings that the entire senior class should not be blamed for what so few had done. In addition, they certainly agreed that to cancel the senior ball was an action far too drastic to fit the crime.

Jim King, senior-class president, tried to talk to the principal and explain how the class felt, but to no avail. The situation became so tense that Jim decided to air grievances with the principal at a senior assembly—called by the class president. When the seniors were all in the auditorium and the principal and vice-principal were seated, Jim walked to the stage and began.

"The senior class wishes to express its thanks to the principal and vice-principal for attending this meeting to hear what we, the senior class, have to say about the incident the night of the banquet, and all that has happened since that time," Jim said, very cautiously and clearly. "We understand the seriousness of the matter, and we do not wish to minimize that fact. We agree that restitution must be made, and we agree that the entire class is in some way responsible for seeing that the matter is handled properly and satisfactorily. However, we do not think that the cancellation of the senior ball is either necessary or appropriate. Since the principal has determined that no matter what the senior class does to compensate for the damages, the ball will not be held, then as senior-class president I wish to inform the principal that our class had decided to hold its own ball—with or without the approval of the principal." It was Rollie who handled the matter, and in a way that pleased both parties; the ball was held with school approval, and with little mention of the tension between parties. Within a year, the principal was fired.

Barbara was convinced, this Saturday morning, that she and the children should leave Iowa as soon as possible and return home. It would be much easier to wait in Keuka than spend any more uncomfortable days here. *It started out such a wonderful vacation,* she thought. *How could it end so dismally?* She knew she and Rollie had a good marriage, but she realized that they needed one another. *It takes something like this,* she thought, *to strengthen a marriage,* and she got up from the side of the pond and headed back to the house. Polly would be upset because Barbara would not say anything to interfere with the friendship that had grown between the Hofstaders and the McCormicks. In time, Polly would learn what had happened, and then she would understand.

When Barbara reached the kitchen door, she smelled coffee perking. She opened the door and was surprised to see Polly standing by the sink stirring some frozen orange juice in a large pitcher.

"Good morning," Barbara said as she closed the door and moved toward the cupboard to take down some juice glasses. "I thought I was the only one who couldn't sleep."

"I heard you get up, and after a half hour or so, when I didn't hear any noise, I decided to come downstairs to see if anything was wrong," and Polly lifted the pitcher onto a coaster at the center of the table. "I knew you were an early riser, but on vacation?"

"It's strange, but this is the first time I can remember having such a tough time getting to sleep," Barbara said as she carried some plates to the table, not thinking at all about whether or not it was time for breakfast. "I don't think I could have slept more than an hour or two." She didn't bother to disturb the pile of plates once she had placed them on the table. The coffee was ready, so she poured a cup for Polly and herself. "Has that ever happened to you?"

"I can't say that it has, at least not like that. I can remember, a few years back, when Mike and I attended a champagne party in the afternoon and by the time I got home I was so sleepy that I went right to bed," responded Polly as she sipped the coffee. "It was only about seven when I dropped off, and I woke up at around three in the morning and couldn't get back to sleep. But I had slept soundly for eight hours, so I suppose that had been all the sleep I needed," she said.

"I agree," said Barbara, "that isn't the same." She fumbled with her cup and continued. "I just don't know why I wasn't at all tired last night. We certainly didn't oversleep yesterday." Barbara did not have to think long about her sleepless night; she knew well why it happened, but she would not reveal it to Polly.

"Polly," Barbara said somewhat pensively, "I think the kids and I will pack and start back today."

"Oh, no," Polly said. "We were going to do some shopping,

and I wanted to show off the new mall. You'd really like the change in this little town."

"No, I think it would be best if we started back. I want to get some things done around the house before Rollie gets home, and that will be sometime before next Saturday. Lake homes have a funny way of piling up work if you stay away too long. Besides, it's so nice by the water, and I am beginning to miss it. The summer is so short, and although it was great to visit you again, I really hate to miss some of the best time of the year at the lake." And Barbara began to think of even more reasons to be home now. "Aliceanne will be leaving for school in less than ten days, and we have a lot to do before she leaves. If it hadn't been a spur-of-the-moment trip out here, we'd never had come this late in the season."

"Barbara, is there something bothering you?" Polly asked, recognizing that Barbara was beginning to build arguments for leaving, which always indicated—at least with Barbara—an uneasiness with her present situation.

"Not really, Polly. It's just that we should get on the road. We've had a lot of fun, and it's been good being together again, but a week now is really all we can afford." Barbara got up from the chair next to the door, placed her empty cup on the counter, and started for her room. It was eight o'clock, so if she could hurry the children—and that was not always possible—she could be on the road within an hour and a half and get some distance covered on the first leg of the trip. Although in the past, she, Rollie and the children had made the trip in one day, today, with the 55 mph limit, it proved to be too much time behind the wheel for one day. She could probably reach Chicago or even South Bend before dark, and the Welches always figured that to be about the halfway point.

"Barbara, I'll fix some breakfast, and sandwiches for the trip," Polly said as she busied herself in the kitchen. "I think the children had something planned for today, so you had better get your arguments ready," Polly cautioned Barbara as she left the room. Polly took things in stride, and if Barbara decided to leave like this, it really did not disturb her. Even when Polly had made plans for a party, the fact that people came or didn't come had little outward effect on her. Polly always seemed to be able to cope with the unusual, and adversity, in the calmest way. In that respect, she was very much like her sister Barbara. Perhaps that was one reason why both their marriages were so stable, why each loved her husband so much—and each husband loved his wife—for both were able to do so many things that pleased their husbands (and children) without apparently diminishing their own pleasure. Their mutual friends often commented on that fact, especially the Hofstaders.

CHAPTER ELEVEN

Sunday was a cold, crisp morning when Rollie got up, but the sun was shining brightly. His room apparently had not been heated through the night, as evidenced by the coldness and dampness of the room and by the condensation that had collected on the window. He got up quickly, drew his robe about him, and opened his door to see if the bathroom was free. He saw a shadow through the glass door to the bathroom, so he stepped back into his room to await his turn at the facilities. He smiled and thought how strange it was that anyone should build such a lovely house, go to the expense of providing the luxury of a shower and sink in each room, yet maintain but one toilet—and with a semitransparent glass door besides! The Irish were strange ones, he thought.

He heard movement outside his door, and that was his cue to once again see if the coast was clear. It was, so he headed quickly down the hall toward the bathroom, intent upon beating anyone else to the door. Once inside, he found the furnishings well made and in keeping with the quality of the bedrooms. *Perhaps when the house is finally completed,* he thought, *they may even find time to install a lock on the bathroom door,* and he started back to his room to get dressed for breakfast.

Everyone must have slept in this morning, since Rollie sat in the dining room until a little after nine before he heard movement in the kitchen. The breakfast was well worth the wait, however, and he ate his favorite meal of the day with relish. The bacon was not served in thick chunks, but care was taken to slice each strip very thin, and the several pieces he chose were lean and crisp. The bread, too, was much finer than usual—and thinner—yet it retained the taste quality that he favored in Irish oatmeal bread. The eggs were light and fluffy, so much so that Rollie could easily have been convinced that an American chef had been engaged. He would leave Mrs. Nic Gearailt with a more positive attitude about Irish breakfast, if that could be possible. By 9:45 A.M., Rollie was on his way, and today he would drive straight to Bantry Bay—through Killarney, of course—and perhaps he might even stop at Muckross Gardens for a bit, for he wanted to see more of the beautiful coastline about which so much had been written. So far, he thought, he had seen a great deal of truth in what he had read, and no matter what beautiful scene one described in words, it could only be improved upon by viewing it. No doubt it was in great part this positive attitude of Rollie's that had provided him with such delightful feelings about Ireland throughout these days of his second visit.

The drive from Baile na nGall to Killarney was even less of a problem than it had been when he arrived the day before. There were very few cars on the road this morning, so Rollie had the view to himself. He chose the southern route out of Dingle through Inch, Aughils and on to Castlemaine. At Castlemaine, he decided not to folow N70 around the Ring of Kerry—he had completed that ride one time before—but instead chose to continue east until he reached N22, which would take him directly south to Killarney. Because the roads were so free of traffic, he was able to make good time and by noon he was in the downtown area of Killarney, where he discovered a parking lot adjacent to the main street. Rollie found it difficult to pass up an opportunity to visit this city, which had been so memorable for him during his three-day stay in '74. He remembered attending church one Sunday (lately, he never thought about church) in Killarney and marveling at how similar this cathedral was to the one Orwell described in *A Clergyman's Daughter,* and the thought of Dorothy and her minister father came to mind. Rollie chuckled to himself today as he recalled these things, and he was pleased with himself that he found it so enjoyable to compare his literary experiences with his actual life experiences; it made the fantasy so much better.

Rollie stayed downtown for only fifteen or twenty minutes and then reclaimed his car and headed for Muchross Abbey and the gardens.

It took Rollie no more than a few minutes to get to the gardens, and this time he did not bother to go through the mansion, but headed immediately for the north side of the estate and the lush, green layout that adorned the several acres that comprised the estate. He once again marveled at the lawn, which gave under each step, and he presumed that there was a great deal of water beneath the turf that made it so springy. It reminded him of the feeling he got as a child when he would stand and jump on his bed, or when he would try to walk from his bed to his brother's and how it was impossible to keep from swaying—or even falling. He did not sway or fall on the Muckross lawn, and certainly the comparison was an exaggeration, but nevertheless it was a feeling on grass that he had never before experienced and suspected would find nowhere else. He crossed the many small bridges that spanned the creek as it wound through the gardens, and he saw the giant flowers, which abounded. He faltered at flower names, but he thought these fuchsia and rhododendrons, and he remembered that similar varieties that grew in America reached only a very small portion of the size he saw here, and that fact he attributed both to the climate and the excessive moisture of Killarney. Rollie had learned, thanks mostly to the instruction and example of Barbara, to spend time observing these wonders of nature, and as a result it was well after two o'clock when he reached his car to continue his journey, remembering that his goal was to spend more time this day on the coast. But, he thought, Muckross was well worth the delay.

Rollie retraced his way to downtown and found the intersection of routes N22 and N71. He turned south on N71, which would take him along the bank of both lower and upper Lough Leane Lake, providing more of the inland beauty that Rollie loved to see. The traffic would begin to get heavier now, since it was well into Sunday afternoon, but this did not bother Rollie as much as it might have had he not been so happy with all that he had seen that day. The roads were not nearly so treacherous as when he drove through Connor Pass, and the slower speed at this point simply left him with more opportunity to observe the sights along the lake. It was still a beautiful afternoon, and the sun seemed to highlight the countryside in just the right spots. The green of Killarney was a contrast to the yellow and gold of the northwest, and this new beauty was just as attractive to Rollie. He said to himself, as he often had done before, that he could not understand why anyone would ever want to leave this beautiful island. And he drove on toward Bantry Bay.

The drive would be short, and soon Rollie could see that coastline that he had quickly grown to love, but he also thought about the more practical question of life in Ireland. It was a fact that most of the people were very poor, some trying hard to eke out a living by working the land, such that it was, and by keeping sheep and goats. Others, living nearer the larger cities, had jobs, which did provide them with income, but wages here were not large and often such jobs provided families with only the bare necessities of life. It was seldom that a family could save anything at all from such wages, and when it was possible, it was such a small amount that it seemed hardly worth the effort. He thought, too, that although his own children were adults, or nearly so, he and Barbara would have a difficult time making a living should they choose to move to Ireland. Rollie was a teacher, but there was little need in this land for more teachers. Fewer and fewer young men and women were choosing to stay at home, mainly because of the poor economic situation in which they found themselves, and consequently the child population of Ireland was continually growing smaller. It was fast becoming a land of old people, as it were, since the only members of the younger generation who remained were those who felt an obligation to continue with the family business, at least whenever that business appeared to retain some stability. And even those young people knew they could never support a family. These businesses, too, were becoming fewer and fewer. And he thought of Barbara and how she did not care for the cold and damp of this country, and of course it was that way all of the time. No, he thought, it is a lovely place to visit, but one must not think at all about trying to build a new life here; perhaps an extended visit would be possible, but certainly not anything more than one could arrange through a sabbatical. And now Rollie was armed with a new idea, one that he had never before considered. At least it was something to think about, and perhaps with the possibility of travel to the Continent so accessible, Barbara might think more favorably about it.

As Rollie became lost in his thoughts, the countryside passed by quickly, so it was not long before he was driving along the narrow roads in Glengarriff, excited by the number of people who appeared to be milling around the sea wall, if one might call it that—although it was not so sturdy as a sea wall might be, nor was it near the water—some talking, others just standing and looking about, mainly at the sidewalk vendors and the various items that were for sale. The drive was so slow that often Rollie was stopped for several minutes at a time because only one lane was open to traffic. There were many tourist buses cluttering the paths, and the parking spaces jutted into the street so that if one were not careful how he parked his car, one end or the other interfered with the westbound lane of traffic, thus causing as big a problem as the buses. But no one seemed to mind, especially the police. (Rollie discovered very quickly that the police in Ireland seldom bothered about such things, especially traffic matters, so he learned not to let it bother him either.) Once through this section of town, Rollie decided to look for lodgings for the night, before he drove the remaining few miles to the bay.

Rollie found a space, luckily, and parked his car. As he had been working his way through the traffic, he had noticed a tourist-board office and decided to secure a room through that service. He had little problem and quickly was on his way to Mrs. Guerin's Sea Front. He found the room traditionally old, but warm and comfortable, and at four pounds for B and B he thought it was acceptable. He told the maid (Mrs. Guerin was out at the moment) that he would return in the evening, and left for the bay.

Within fifteen minutes, Rollie got an excellent view of the bay, but it was another ten to fifteen minutes before he found any place where he might park his car and venture on foot to the shore. When he finally parked in an area provided for such visits, he stood and looked at the hills that surrounded this section of the bay. Although he was not at all disappointed with the view he got as he entered from the east, he believed that the view from the west was more spectacular, and he climbed a large hill to get a better look. He walked about three-quarters of a mile before he turned to see, once again, Bantry Bay. It was beautiful, he thought, but probably not more so than from the east. He wondered why he had become so conscious of the angle of view; this kind of thing had never before even crossed his mind. "I am becoming a true artist," he said out loud and proceeded to descend the hill. He spent some time on the shore looking for interesting rocks and snails. He collected some small pieces that he thought would make good souvenirs, put them in the car, and walked across the street to the Bantry Hotel, where he found an attractive dining room and a very comfortable bar. He entered the bar and ordered a glass of lager and inquired about dinner and whether or not it was served in the bar. He could order sandwiches in the bar, so that is what he did. His food, although unimaginative, was sufficient, but the atmosphere was excellent. All of the chairs in the bar were backed with soft leather, and one simply got lost within the cushions. It was a completely relaxing experience and one that Rollie had not encountered in a bar prior to this time. He judged that there must have been other bars as comfortable, but he earnestly believed that this one was unique. Of course, he would never be able to prove this thesis, but if he could not encounter a bar like this one during the remainder of his trip, then he would leave Ireland with the story—and firm belief—that Bantry Hotel Bar would provide the traveler with a unique experience in comfort. And whether or not his story was fact, it remained a good story to tell.

Rollie was in no hurry tonight, so he took his time and was surprised to discover that he had spent three hours eating and drinking in the bar. Much of that time he was engaged in conversation with the various waitresses who came and went as well as virtually all of the customers. The topic of his conversation ranged from the nature of Bantry Bay and what it was to work in the hotel and impressions of guests and travelers to brief mention of topography and stories of the sea. Rollie had learned much about the customs of the Irish through his familiarity with the works of Walter Macken, and he felt as though he could carry on an intelligent conversation with the natives about such things of which the usual traveler (at least, Rollie thought so) would have little or no knowledge. When Rollie talked, he was not boring, and even the casual traveler was interested in what he said and the questions he asked. He discovered that people enjoyed talking to him, and in fact, many of the Irish were glad to talk to a foreigner who had some knowledge about their country and customs. In just these few days he had been in Ireland, Rollie was understood, and he understood the Irish well. Perhaps the strong positive feelings he was building, day by day, about this second trip came as much from the beauty he observed as from the ease with which he managed to get along with the Irish.

It was dark by the time Rollie left the Bantry Hotel and walked to the parking lot across the street. He fumbled in his pocket for the keys to the car, but could not find them. He searched all his pockets, but they were not there. He went back to the bar and asked the bartender if he had the keys or if anyone had given him a set that may have been left. The bartender answered in the negative, but before Rollie had time to become upset about the situation, he caught the glimmer of something shiny beside the booth where he had been eating his supper. Luck was with him, for these were the keys. He thanked the bartender (who, in fact had been no help at all) for his help and again left the bar and walked to the car. He promised himself that he would be careful, and as he tried to open the car door, he dropped the keys. *So much for that promise,* he thought. Rollie quickly picked them up and opened the door. Within seconds, he was headed toward Glengariff and the Sea Front Hotel, thinking already of a sound night's sleep and the prospect of a marvelous tomorrow. How many marvelous tomorrows could there be? He chuckled to himself as he drove straight to his room.

When Rollie had first inspected his room at the Sea Front, he had not noticed that it looked out over the bay, or, at least, one little inlet from the sea. Tonight that view could not be missed, with the lights indicating several boats on that inlet. *Tomorrow,* he thought, *I shall be out on that bay,* and he stared at the lights and the stillness of the water. It was inviting him, and he would accept the invitation. He still had until Wednesday to reach Dublin, so there was no reason to hurry and miss this attraction of the south.

As he lay in bed this Sunday night, Rollie quickly reviewed all that had happened during the past eight days and was pleased that they had been so filled with such a variety of activities and with a new knowledge and understanding of the Irish people. He was pleased, too, at how he had changed and that he now could appreciate things of nature so much better than ever before had seemed possible. He had always enjoyed beautiful places and meeting interesting people, but only for a very short time; beauty was on the golf course, for example, where people and things were as interesting as playing well. *But now,* he thought, *it is different; I know I have changed tremendously during these past eight days.* And while he was trying to convince himself of how much he had changed, Barbara flashed into his mind and he wondered what she and the children were doing. His thoughts, however, were self-centered; not for a moment did he entertain the possibility of writing or calling home. It was as though his association with America and his family and home were changed, too, and that this present experience had become more the reality. He did not want to think about home, and in an attempt to stop this train of thought, he pulled the covers over his head and fell asleep.

The Glengariff visit provided more for Rollie than he had expected. He awoke on Monday morning with the smell of fresh coffee and frying bacon, a certain motivator for Rollie Welch. He washed and dressed quickly, then descended to the small dining room below. As usual, tables were set, and he chose a single near the window and again (as usual!) ate heartily. When he had finished, he thanked his hostess, took his single bag to the car, and sat there wondering what to do this morning. He noticed the sign advertising rides to the Garnish Island, so he left the car in place and walked to the dock ticket house to make inquiries.

"Pardon me," he said, "but what is the attraction on Garnish Island?"

"The Gardens," came the reply from the rough-shaven captain, or at least Rollie thought him a captain.

"Is that a tourist attraction?" Rollie asked.

"Call it what you will," the man said, "but it's pretty sensational."

"What's the price?" Rollie asked as he began to create an inner excitement about a possible visit.

"Fifty pence round trip, but it's an extra fifty pence to enter. They sell tickets at the entrance—on the island," the captain replied, now getting a little irritated with Rollie because a line was beginning to form and Rollie was holding up progress. Rollie noticed the people behind him and realized what he was doing. Since he so recently had prided himself on how much he was not like the usual tourist, he felt immediate embarrassment. He made his decision quickly.

Rollie took the trip and was astonished at what he saw. Gardens they were, and many varieties. He had learned that until about 1925 the island was barren. At that time, the Bryce family planted it with trees, shrubs, and hundreds of flowers, which grew rapidly and flourished, mainly because of the Gulf Stream, which kept the island warm the year round. Rollie saw flowering shrubs and plants from the Himalayas, China, South America, South Africa, and Tasmania, as well as sections of gardens that displayed the flowers and other plants of Japan and Italy. There were hundreds of visitors that day, and all could not help but marvel at the spectacle. Rollie spent easily four or five hours wandering through the gardens, houses, and several of the other structures that could be found throughout this rather small spot. The ferry left every half-hour, so he did not worry about his ride to the mainland—or—more correctly stated—the larger island! The day was somewhat overcast, but the sun did shine occasionally, so the beauty of the gardens was not diminished.

For a moment during his walk through the Italian Garden, Rollie thought how nice it would be if no one but Anna were here with him and they could enjoy this experience together, two lovers of nature, mature people who recognized and understood beauty, and then he put that thought out of his mind, with difficulty. Why should he, a happily married man, have these thoughts? Yet they kept returning. It was difficult for him to blank Anna from his mind today. Three or four days ago, it was much easier. Perhaps subsconsciously he was preparing for Wednesday, when he knew he would see her, or at least he planned to see her, although he had not made any specific plans. By two o'clock, Rollie had returned to his car at the Sea Front. As he buckled his seat belt and started the engine, the Garnish Island had already been forgotten, and he could only think about Wednesday—and Anna.

CHAPTER TWELVE

As Rollie drove toward Cork on Monday afternoon, he was unaware that in Dublin, Anna was thinking about him and mentally preparing for his visit on Wednesday. Whatever feeling Rollie had for Anna, she now seemed to be developing a similar one toward him. Anna had spent a delightful day or two in Cork with Jack, as she had spent so many other wonderful times with him during the past year. It was true that she enjoyed the company of Jack a great deal and had dated him exclusively for the past eight or nine months, but she never had entertained any thoughts about marriage. The feelings this afternoon were different than those she had for Jack and, at least for the present, demanded more of her attention.

Anna thought of Rollie as a good husband, a responsible father, and a genuine intellectual. She remembered their conversation of Myra's party and smiled as she thought of all the topics they had covered within a few hours and how excited Rollie had become when they discussed fictional characters. Together they espoused a philosophy of literature, as Rollie had termed it, that made the two of them "literaturally compatible," a term that Rollie had invented and a label that he gave to anyone who would discuss literature at great length. Anna had laughed at him that night when he gave her the label, thinking it more the result of his drinking so much Paddy than of his recognition of her wide knowledge in literary matters. But this afternoon, she decided that Rollie had been serious and that the two of them did seem to have a mutual respect for literary genius.

Anna had taken this afternoon off and was sitting in her living room listening to the stereo and wondering what Rollie might like to do on Wednesday, since it would be his last night in Ireland. She wondered if it would be presumptuous of her to arrange a little gathering for the evening. Since there would be only four of them at most, all could come to her place that night. Yet she thought that kind of arrangement might not be to Rollie's liking, so she decided to call Myra for a suggestion.

"Myra, this is Anna. How are you?" she said.

"Anna, how nice to hear from you. I'm fine, and you?" Myra was genuinely interested.

"I'm just fine, Myra. Do you know that Rollie will be in Dublin on Wednesday?" Anna asked.

"No! Oh, it's too bad James won't be here," Myra responded.

"Well," Anna continued, "I thought we might do something on Wednesday, since Rollie will be leaving for London—and then home—on Thursday. We probably won't get to see him for quite a while after that."

"Would you like to come to the house?" Myra offerred.

"What would you think if you, Jack, and I asked Rollie to the apartment?" Anna asked. "It would be a bit easier for him to find my place, I suspect, than yours."

"That sounds fine," said Myra, "and what can I bring?"

"Let me prepare this one," said Anna. "You've done too many already!" She laughed, which somehow convinced Myra of Anna's desire to be hostess this time.

"All right, then. What time shall I be there?"

"Eight o'clock," responded Anna, "and be prepared for a smashing farewell!" Anna hung up the phone and sat back in her chair, pleased that she had made the call and even more pleased that Rollie would have a fine send-off on Wednesday.

It was only Monday, but already Anna started to arrange the room and tidy up a bit, although her place seldom could be found in disarray. Anna had been to so many of Myra and James's parties that had been so successful, and she wanted this one—her first—to be a good first effort! She now wondered what to prepare and how much whiskey to buy. She knew that everyone drank Paddy, but she also knew that Myra seldom drank even one drink when she had to drive. Too, Jack often wanted a lager rather than whiskey, especially when he had important business the following day. Since this party would take place on Wednesday, Jack most likely would be obligated the following day. Then Anna wondered if dinner might be appropriate. That would minimize the drinking, yet would keep them together for a long time that evening. And she had to consider the fact that she, too, would be working the next morning and that a lot of drinking was out of the question. With just the right kind of preparation, all could have a good time on Wednesday, get in a lot of talk, yet still be in fine shape the next morning. Anna whispered to herself that it was a good thing that James was away; he didn't know how to have a "moderate" drinking evening. Anna had known James for almost a year now, and she had never seen him show any ill effect of drinking, despite the fact that he seldom came home from work without stopping for three or four drinks beforehand—to say nothing of the drinking he could do at parties. And he seemed always either to be attending them or to be giving them! Anna laughed when she thought what fun James was at these parties, and she frowned, just a bit, to think that he would not be at this one.

Although there were few jobs in Ireland for the young adults, those few who had the appropriate education could find work. Anna was one of these few. After she had finished her B.A. in the states, she came to Ireland and was fortunate to get a job as accountant with the new McDonald's Restaurant that was attempting to establish itself on the Island. Anna generally worked a regular 9:00 A.M. to 5:00 P.M. day, but she was not restricted to those hours and, in fact, often varied them to enable her to be with Jack. It was as though McDonald's had hired her as an independent accountant, but retained her on the regular payroll. This situation suited Anna, for she was a person who would never long allow herself to be "boxed in" by regular hours. She was, in her own terms, a free spirit and wished to remain so. Not only did she apply this spirit to her work, but also to her life, which was the reason that on this afternoon she allowed herself to think this way about Rollie. Her relationship with all of her friends was like this, and she never understood why anyone should feel slighted if she happened to direct her attention more to one than another, since she refused to allow herself to become "attached" to anyone; to her, even the relationship with Jack was not at all serious. And Jack was an excellent choice for her partner, since he looked for no permanent attachments; Jack was happy to have a lovely girl friend who liked to be with him and who made no demands of him. The relationship was a good one for both of them.

Anna had severed her relationship with home and family. After her education in a conservative, but exclusive women's college, she had left her comfortable parents' home and established residence in Ireland. Throughout the four years, her parents seldom saw her—or for that matter, did they wish to see her. She had been an only and unwanted child who upset the life of her parents and consequently never was able to fit into their plans. Her vacations from school were always spent traveling, since her parents gave whatever money was necessary to keep her busy—away from home. Her parents were wealthy, each in his own right, and her father, in addition to his inherited wealth, had a very successful realty business. It was a strange family, especially when one discovered how little concern the parents had for their daughter, but it was so. Anna was given whatever money could buy, so when she decided to live in Ireland it was never a question of whether or not she could afford it. But, as fortune would have it, she found employment immediately and managed to live, fairly comfortably, without depending upon her parents' money. And Anna had learned, as a very young child, not to depend upon her parents for emotional support, but to look to herself for all such fulfillment. This fact may have accounted for the ease with which she made friends and for the fact that she had not made any serious commitments in her relationships, especially with men. It was unlike her, then, to think this way about Rollie.

Anna did not call Jack this afternoon to tell him about Wednesday evening. They had already made tentative plans to be together Wednesday, so she knew that this arrangement would be acceptable to him. Occasionally during the past months when Anna and Jack had been dating, last-minute changes had been made and they had never disturbed either party. But as Anna thought more about Wednesday evening, she grew excited. She even began to feel nervous—about what she did not know, but nervous nevertheless. It was a good feeling and one that Anna had not experienced in a long time.

Anna lived two blocks from St. Patrick's Cathedral, on the extension of Crumlin Road. (When she had told Myra that her location would be easier for Rollie to find, she had thought that Rollie would approach Dublin from Naas Road.) It was still afternoon, so she decided to shop for some things for Wednesday evening. *Biscuits and cheese, a bottle of Paddy, and some lager should do well, at least for starters,* she thought. Preparations for dinner could wait until tomorrow. And full of happiness in anticipation of a wonderful reunion, she set about her dutiful rounds!

Later on Monday evening, Jack called Anna to confirm their date for Wednesday. When he discovered what Anna had planned, he was very agreeable and told Anna he would be there about 7:00 P.M. Jack also told her to count on him for the entrée: four sirloin steaks, cut American style. The Irish like their meat, usually boiled. Whenever they ate steaks, the meat was always cut about ½ inch thick and fried, well done. Jack had learned from Anna that Americans preferred the thick cut, and the more he tried it that way, the better he liked it. This gesture, then, was as much a favor to himself as it was an attempt to please the "American."

"Don't forget to insist upon 1½ inches," Anna said, "and then you can count upon them being at least 1 inch."

"Sean is a friend, Anna, so he'll cut them the way I ask," answered Jack.

"But remember the last time . . . " Anna started.

"I've taught him since then," Jack interrupted. "I also threatened to cut off his whiskey supply."

"You're right. That should do it," Anna said, smiling as she did. Sean was quite a legend; it was difficult to remember the last time one could not smell liquor on his breath. But he was a good butcher—and reasonable—so Jack always bought his meat from him.

"Is there anything else I can help with?" Jack asked, thinking that he might also pick up the drink.

"Thanks, Jack, but I've already got some whiskey and lager, and I can't think of anything else. We should have a good time."

"Aye, we should," answered Jack. "I'll be seeing you, then, tomorrow evening."

"Good-bye, love," said Anna, and she hung up the phone. The remainder of the evening was spent arranging and rearranging furniture and thinking about the good time they would have. Anna also thought about her job and matters to attend to in the morning, and with these thoughts she went to bed.

On Tuesday morning, Anna woke early, at least for someone who normally gets to work at 9:30 A.M. By eight o'clock, she had dressed and breakfasted, allowing her much more time than usual to get to work. She spent some time doing the few dishes she used for breakfast and then sat down to read a section of yesterday's paper that she had not finished. She noticed an article describing an auto accident just outside Cork, and by the description of the incident, she suddenly thought of Rollie. She was relieved when the article identified the victim, an Italian on holidays; she was sad, of course, for him and his family, but glad it was not Rollie. She thought she had better stop reading the paper; she did not want any more coincidences to occur. Anna gave one last look in the hall mirror and left for work.

Just outside the apartment, Jack was waiting. Jack was aware of Anna's habit of leaving her apartment about 8:45 A.M. and leisurely walking to the bus stop. Anna never drove to work, because of the difficulty finding parking space, and it was rare when she missed the nine o'clock bus. Whenever he had time, Jack would pick her up and both would stop for a cup of coffee before she started work.

"Good morning," Anna said as she opened the car door and settled into the front seat.

"And good morning to you," answered Jack in a very pleasant morning voice. "Where would such a lovely be heading this morning?" Jack said as he pretended Anna was a hitchhiker.

"Wherever you're headed," Anna replied, continuing the hoax.

"A cup of coffee, then?" and Jack drove off to the restaurant.

"Not too busy today?" asked Anna.

"Got an appointment at ten, but plenty of free time before that," said Jack. "A supplier with a new line wants to convince me to carry the product, but I'm not too interested. However, it can't hurt to listen. He'll probably take me to lunch, so I'll listen a while for that."

"When's the last time you paid for lunch?" Anna asked.

"I'm always buying lunch and dinner," Jack said. "Don't you remember Cork? That cost me a few pence."

"I also remember you saying that the company would pay for those expenses," Anna answered.

"Well, a small detail." And by the time the conversation reached this point, they had arrived at the restaurant.

Jack and Anna sat for a few moments without saying anything. Anna started the conversation by asking Jack about Rollie.

"What do you think of him?" she asked, wondering if Jack had formed any opinion at all, if Rollie had made any impression.

"Seems a nice chap," Jack answered, not offering any indication of feeling about him.

"Do you think he's stuffy?" asked Anna. She remembered Jack commenting on a number of associates who carried on what he termed insufferable banter about the latest plays, paintings, and all, as if to impress one with their intelligence.

"Can't say, really. I haven't talked with him for more than a few minutes. Remember, I didn't go to dinner with you at Snaffles," Jack said.

"But you must have heard a lot of what we were talking about at Myra's," said Anna. "The living room is very small, and all of us were in there."

"Well, he was a guest who was drinking heavily," said Jack, " and I shouldn't judge a man under those conditions."

"Do you think he's genuine—I mean knowledgeable—about the things he says?" Anna asked, pushing Jack to make known his judgment about Rollie.

"You should know more than I," said Jack. "He was talking about those special interests of yours—and you know we don't talk much about literature."

"Do you like him, Jack?" Anna asked.

"Really can't say, one way or another. He dresses well," and Jack smiled, knowing that he was successful in not letting Anna know what he felt about Rollie. Jack realized that Anna had some special interest in Rollie, and he was not about to help her make a decision.

"Jack, will you pick me up after work?" Anna asked. "We could get a bite somewhere."

"Fine," Jack answered. "Five be all right?" Jack knew that Anna could work as long as she wished.

"I'll see you then," she said. "And thanks, Jack."

Throughout the day, Anna thought about Jack and Rollie. She found herself comparing the two; never before had she done anything like this. She had always been able to accept people as they were; whatever qualities one had were fine, and those qualities never reflected upon or interfered with her acceptance of others. Yet today, on the eve of her first party—she called it that—she found herself thinking about these two men: one who was married, the other who had clearly expressed the opinion that he was not ready for any commitment to another. Jack was an intelligent man, witty and charming, always ready to have a good time. He did not drink heavily, like James, for example, but drank enough to have fun. He loved parties; he loved to be out with people. Jack seldom talked about reflective subjects; he preferred to sing and dance, and if one must talk, then about Irish football or a little politics. Anyway, parties were for action and activity, not talking, and Jack never turned down an invitation to get with James. His college association with James appeared to have left an indelible mark.

Rollie was also a gentleman, but very much unlike Jack. He seemed to desire to withdraw from the crowd, to talk very personally with another. What Jack found exciting conversation, Rollie found exasperating. Beauty, life, art—those were the things so precious, those were the things to talk about, upon which to reflect. And Rollie was exciting; his talk of the great men and women of literature betrayed a genuine admiration and almost adoration of their accomplishments. It was infectious, and Anna had caught the disease, as was so very apparent whenever she had been with him. She thought about her telephone conversations with him, and despite the fact that Rollie could not detect it, Anna was again filled with that infectious spirit. And now she would host a small party, and she would, she knew well, look at both men very carefully. This had not been her plan, but Anna was helpless to change anything. Nor did Jack and Rollie suspect they would be on display to a very, very small audience.

Tuesday evening provided an excellent opportunity for Anna to relax and think of other things. Jack had been invited to dinner, so when he called Anna he told her about the invitation and that their "bite" for supper would be a seven o'clock date at the Bailey. The Bailey was just a few hundred yards from McDonald's, but Jack knew that Anna would want to go home and change. He dropped her off and arranged to pick her up again at 6:30 P.M. They would meet the other couple in the pub downstairs.

That evening was a typical Jack and Anna affair, with singing, drinking, and laughing. From time to time, especially after dinner, the couple who were with Jack and Anna got separated in the pub, and, through the raucousness of it all, one searched for the other. The Bailey pub was always that way! Anna and Jack never had a serious word all evening, yet both were pleased with one another's presence and each had an excellent time. Anna never once thought about "her" two men; nor did she think about the following night. The whole evening went on as though nothing had happened, in the past week, anything in this city, in this relationship. And when Jack finally took Anna home at 11:30 P.M., he stopped, as usual, for a short while. Anna made a cup of instant coffee (she only used instant at times like these!), and by 12:15 A.M. Jack had kissed her good night and was on his way home, as if nothing would ever disrupt such a lovely relationship. When Jack had gone, Anna placed the two cups in the sink, filled them with water, and went to her room. She undressed, put on her snugglies, brushed her teeth, and sat on the side of her bed. As she reached to put out the light, she sighed, then slipped under the covers and waited for tomorrow.

CHAPTER THIRTEEN

Rollie's trip from Glengariff to Dublin was relatively uneventful. On Monday afternoon, he drove to Cork for supper, then on to Youghal for the night. He got up early on Tuesday morning and left the guest house before breakfast. Rollie still wanted to revisit a few places, and he knew that Tuesday would give him his last opportunity to do so. Although he would not be sailing until Thursday, he had not yet booked passage and he would need Wednesday in Dublin to take care of that matter.

As Rollie left Youghal and headed east toward Waterford, he encountered an old woman walking along the side of the road. He stopped and asked if she would like a ride. She got into the car, thanked him (he thought!), and rode with him for about ten miles. He had difficulty understanding her, although she spoke English. As far as Rollie could make out, she took this route to Dungarvan about three times a week, sometimes getting a ride, but most of the time walking both ways. She explained that she was visiting her mother, and Rollie wondered how old her mother must have been, since she herself looked to be about ninety! She told him she had been walking for twenty years. She and her husband, who had been dead for fifteen years, had had a small farm in the country, but never had enough money to buy a horse, much less a car. Besides, neither one knew anything about driving an automobile, so what was the sense? Rollie judged she had a lot of sense and wondered if he started walking would he live to be ninety. The old lady was pleasant company, especially since Rollie had had very little company after having left Dublin. Rollie talked with her for about fifteen minutes, but this information was all he could manage. When they got to Dungarvin, Rollie let her out by the side of the road, where she thanked him, waved good-bye, and walked off.

Rollie had left Youghal about seven o'clock, so it was shortly before 9:00 A.M. when he arrived at Waterford. He drove to the waterfront area and found a parking place. Nearby, he found a restaurant, where he ordered breakfast. He enjoyed it, but he thought it was not nearly so nice as he would have received had he eaten at the guest house, especially when he considered the pound ten he was charged. (The cost, however, did include two scones for his trip, and these items would not have been part of his breakfast in Youghal!) Rollie finished eating and went outside to look around. People were beginning to move about, and the streets were filling with visitors. Rollie had never found Waterford an exciting or a beautiful place, and so, after a quick look about, he went back to his car to resume his journey. He had his sights set on Cashel, and he wanted to get there before noon. The day was clear, and Rollie believed he would encounter no problems on the way, but he wanted time, just to be sure.

By eleven-twenty, Rollie could see the Friary atop the Rock of Cashel, and he grew excited at the expectation of wandering through the ruins. On his last visit, the day was so windy, rainy, and cold that Barbara and the children were unwilling to go any farther than just inside the doors of the Friary. Although visitors were being shown through the ruins, there had been a half-hour wait for the next tour, and the cold was just too much for them. This time, Rollie wanted to discover what he had missed.

The visit was pleasing to Rollie, just as so many other visits throughout the island had been. He did his dreaming, he recalled other pleasant sights, and he became completely enthralled with this sight. For the moment, nothing else could have been better. Of course, that is the way it is with such a romantic: one believes what is presently being enjoyed is better than anything else. Rollie, the true romantic, left Cashel with yet another memorable experience, which he someday would recount to his grandchildren—and even about this possibility he romanticized.

From Cashel, the remainder of the trip to Dublin would be quite easy. Rollie would follow the northeast route, N8, to

Portlaoise and at that point take N7 east to Dublin. Once he got to Naas, he would be on the divided highway, and that would get him to Dublin within forty-five minutes. However, he still was in no great hurry to get to Dublin, for he wished to visit the falconry in Robertstown, just north of Naas. Rollie was not a birder nor did he care much about watching exotic birds, but he did remember seeing a large bird once, described to him as an osprey, and the size of that fowl had amazed him. Barbara had reminded him, before he left on this trip, about the hawks and falcons in Robertstown, and he thought he would enjoy seeing these birds at arm's length.

Rollie was not disappointed with his little diversion that afternoon, although Robertstown was difficult to find despite the fact that it was only six to seven miles just north of Naas. He first needed directions to Naas: one sign to Robertstown pointed north, the other west. Upon inquiry, he discovered that either route would have led him to his destination, and this reminded him of the directions he had received in Dingle. There was no direct road, but a series of turns and little country paths, hardly large enough for his car, which eventually got him to the canal just outside the hotel. He could see the enclosure for the birds, but was undecided about where to enter. Had it not been for a few visitors leaving the area, it might have taken Rollie another fifteen or twenty minutes to find the entrance. However, they were obliging enough to point it out to him, and after parking his car in the area provided for visitors—an area almost inaccessible to the falconry—he entered the grounds.

There was nothing at all attractive about this sanctuary—much different from, for example, Muckross Gardens—but simply a cinder path that wound around and through the grounds. There were many small houses provided for the birds, and as Rollie walked through the area, birds were equally inside and outside these houses. A small fence separated the birds from the onlookers, and although each bird was tethered, in some cases it was possible for anyone to approach a bird, well within its ability to attack. When Rollie first entered, for example, the caretaker had a red tail hawk perched on his arm as he showed it to a group of visitors. Shortly after that, the caretaker tossed a piece of raw meat to the bird, and visitors could watch as it tore at the meat. Rollie thought it could do quite a job on someone, if it had the opportunity. As he walked on, he saw many varities of owl, and he was overwhelmed with the snowy, which was the largest owl he had ever seen. This bird was in a cage by itself, and as it flew back and forth, Rollie estimated a wingspan of about six feet. In addition to the owls, he saw birds whose names he had never heard and whose size he had never imagined. As he thought about it, he was glad that they were afraid of him, because he was certainly afraid of them! As he left the falconry and started toward Dublin, he found it almost impossible to believe that these creatures were flying around in the wild—some even around here! Or at least other birds just like these. He smiled as he thought how squirmish he was around a house parakeet or the garden blue jay. He would never go camping again!

As Rollie drove along Naas Road, he thought of the '74 trip and the very fine accommodations he and the family had had at the Green Isle Motel. He also remembered that the city bus line terminated at the Green Isle. Since he must give up his auto before Thursday, Rollie decided to see if he could rent a single at the Green Isle for two nights. The motel was probably only twenty or thirty minutes down the highway, and if he could not get a room there, then there would be plenty of time to try nearer the city center.

Rollie had no difficulty at the Green Isle and was very pleased that he could get a room much nearer the dining room, an arrangement that allowed him to move from his room to the bar and dining room without the necessity of going outdoors. He emptied the car of both pieces of luggage, the first time he had done that since renting the car, and left them in the room while he took the car into town. He had decided to turn it back to the agency today, since he would not be journeying anywhere but to Dublin for the next day and a half and the city bus could take him wherever he desired to go. Besides, the company would refund any overpayment, and that money would be enough to bus him anywhere during the remainder of his stay.

It was only 5:30 P.M. by the time Rollie had returned to the Green Isle, so he decided to nap a bit before going to dinner. He had traveled quite a distance this afternoon, and he was a little weary. He had found the auto agency with no difficulty, left the car there, and caught the Naas Road bus just outside of the entrance to the agency. In all, the operation took him less than an hour. Even the ride back to the motel was pleasant, for he had left just ahead of the afternoon traffic and crowded buses.

As he lay on the bed looking at the ornate light fixture, which seemed so out of place in such a modern motel, Rollie thought that he might pass up the opportunity to see Anna again. Certainly he would call Myra and James and invite both of them—and Pat, too—to America, but he thought it would be best for all if he forgot about Anna. *This whole situation should never have happened,* he thought. It was a lovely idea that James and Myra had introduced him to some friends, and should he again come to Ireland, there would be these others whom he could contact. But there was absolutely no reason to tempt fate; he was happily married, and getting home to Barbara was now important. He began feeling guilty for not having written to Barbara, but by Saturday he would be on his way home to the lake to be reunited with his family, the trip behind him—not forgotten, certainly, but put in its proper perspective. Rollie remembered that he had said he would call Anna, but he knew she did not wait by the telephone for his call, and, for that matter, he didn't remember saying when he would call. He knew that Anna had Jack, and that was as it should have been. He remembered the conversation in Galway, how Anna insisted upon including Jack in every aspect of their conversation, and this fact allowed him to believe that the promised call was not important. Yes, she would be hurt a bit, but not so much that a party the next night could not erase. This eased his mind, and for about an hour and a half, Rollie slept comfortably.

The signs in the lobby of the motel indicated there would be a floor show that evening, so when Rollie awoke at seven o'clock he called the dining room for a reservation to be certain that he had a place for the show. After having taken care of those arrangements, he showered and dressed for dinner. He stopped by the dining room to alert the mâitre d' that he was going to the bar and that he would return in about half an hour. The Green Isle Motel was an interesting place, having a separate grill just off the bar area and a cocktail bar situated two rooms behind the dining room, but Rollie preferred to have his first drink in the bar. He wanted a martini, but, remembering his experience at the Prince of Wales, he ordered a Paddy. There wasn't an Irishman alive who would have trouble with that order. The drink was refreshing, and after finishing one, Rollie tipped the bartender and returned to the dining room. The mâitre d' showed him to his table, and, once seated, Rollie ordered another Paddy. He really wanted that martini, but he knew well what would happen if he ordered it. *But then, Paddy isn't so bad,* he thought and proceeded to have two more before dinner.

Rollie's dinner of veal that evening was excellent. Of all the places he had dined in Ireland, this dining room had served the best food, at least for Rollie's taste. Perhaps it tended to be more American than other places, although the menu was more European than American. Rollie thought that perhaps the preparation was more American, since he had veal at several other places and it had never measured up to the veal at the Green Isle. Of course, topping off dinner with Irish coffee always had a salutary effect, and the Irish coffee tonight was excellent. Rollie was fascinated by the way the waiter made it. He rolled a cart near Rollie's table and proceeded to take ingredients from it. He first warmed the glasses over a small butane torch, being very careful to touch only the stem of the glass. Next the waiter poured hot coffee about ¾ of the way up the glass. Following that operation, he poured a generous portion of whiskey, being very careful to try not to mix the ingredients, but laying one layer of liquid on top of the other. Finally he poured cream down the side of the glass, again being careful that it lay on top of the whiskey. The resultant taste was excellent, and if it had not been for the fact that Rollie had had so many Paddys before dinner, he would have been tempted to take a second coffee. As it was, he drank slowly, and that drink lasted him through the floor show.

Rollie did not wait for a second show, but instead returned to the bar for a nightcap. Halfway there, he changed his mind and decided to retire for the night. As on so many occasions during the past few days, he had driven his car quite a lot, and he was tired. The short nap he had taken before dinner seemed only to help him remember how comfortable the bed was, and thus it was easy for him to skip the drink tonight and get to bed. Although he did not have many things to take care of on Wednesday, he did want to be certain to get his booking early in the day and then to do some shopping on O'Connell Street. He took little care getting undressed, dropped his coat and pants on a chair, flipped off his shoes without untying the strings, snuggled into bed, socks and all, and fell asleep almost instantly. That night he dreamed of a new experience: taking the boat to England.

Rollie awoke on Wednesday morning about eight o'clock, feeling a little stale from the night before, but not so much that he had lost his appetite. He looked forward to a large breakfast, which, in fact, he got in his room this morning. Rollie had never tried room service for a meal, and this would probably be his last opportunity to order breakfast at such a reasonable rate. (There was only a charge for service; the food came with the price of the room.) One need not go into detail here, but be assured that what he was served could not be topped by any other breakfast he had eaten on this trip. Rollie was happy to know that the place he liked best on his '74 trip was still—by far—the best accommodation of this trip. Some things—good ones—just don't change! Rollie did not hurry this morning, despite his anxiety concerning the booking, for he knew the bus would get him to the office well before noon—and that was time enough.

After Rollie had finished his breakfast, he put the tray outside his door and walked to the back of the motel to wait for the bus. He was fortunate that Wednesday was another sunny day; he had had his share of sunny days on this trip! Within minutes, the bus arrived. Rollie was the only passenger from the Green Isle this morning, so during the three- or four-minute stop, Rollie talked with the bus driver. Although the conversation was anything but profound, Rollie did discover that the golf club across the street from the motel was private, but that visitors were allowed, on occasion, to play it. Rollie also wanted to know about the collection of fares.

"Why is it," Rollie asked, "you take the passenger's word for his destination?"

"Well, they know where they are going, now, don't they?" the bus driver answered, smiling, but not insultingly so.

"That's true," said Rollie, "but how do you know they're telling the truth?" This question of truth had always bothered Rollie.

"Why would they lie?" the bus driver questioned.

"I don't know," said Rollie, "but people do sometimes."

"I suppose. But they've no reason on the bus. I can see where they get off," the driver said, motioning to the door of the bus, which opened just to his left.

"Can you remember all of the people when the bus is filled?" Rollie continued.

"Well, I have another man to help," he answered, really avoiding the question.

"And what about those people who board the bus, take a seat on the upper level, and get off without paying you?" Rollie really wanted to have that question answered.

"They wouldn't leave without paying," the driver responded, looking, a bit perplexed, at Rollie.

"You mean that no one ever gets on and off without paying?" Rollie asked, as if to affirm the ridiculousness of any such possibility.

"Do you know someone who had?" asked the driver.

"No, I don't," said Rollie, "but I can't ride all the buses to check and see!" Rollie was starting to become exasperated.

"I don't either," the driver responded and at that point had already left the Green Isle and was beginning to collect passengers along the way. Rollie realized, by this time, that he was not going to get the negative response he had expected, so he ended the question-and-answer session and turned to view what he could on the ride to O'Connell Street.

Throughout this trip, Rollie had had ample opportunities to view situations worth remembering, and the ride this morning to Dublin produced yet another. Shortly after the bus had arrived at the Green Isle, a second driver, or conductor, boarded the bus. This was the helper to which the driver had referred. At one stop along the way, several visitors, probably American, boarded the bus and sat down. The conductor went from seat to seat taking money and dispensing tickets, and when he reached a young boy who had just boarded, he engaged in a short conversation.

"Twenty pence," the boy said. It was customary for the regulars to indicate the price rather than the destination. Some of the visitors who traveled the line with regularity soon discovered this habit and imitated the natives.

"Please?" said the conductor.

The boy repeated, "Twenty pence," and held out a fifty pence coin, expecting the conductor to take it and make change.

"Please?" repeated the conductor, and Rollie could see that the boy was becoming confused.

"O'Connell Street," the boy said, reverting to naming the destination, hoping that strategy would clarify the matter.

"O'Connell Street, please," said the conductor, and the boy smiled and said, "Please!" Rollie had been confused a bit, too, but was heartened to see that someone still cared about manners. He wondered how well that procedure would work on a bus in New York City.

Rollie got off the bus on O'Connell Street where it is intersected by the river Liffey. He turned right and headed toward the Custom House Quay, figuring he would find a boat-booking agency somewhere in that vicinity. It was now about 11:00 A.M., a perfect time, he thought, since the people would have been at work for about 1½ hours, yet had a full hour before they would leave for lunch. He was correct about finding an agency, and within ten minutes he was engaged in conversation with a young man who seemed more interested in providing Rollie with the best possible accommodations at the lowest price.

"I suppose second class would be sufficient," said Rollie, "since the ride is only three hours at most."

"Sir, that's true, but for only an additional three pounds you can secure first class and cabin," the agent proposed.

"First class would be fine, but I really don't think it's necessary," Rollie answered, a little irritated that the agent would continue to try to sell him something he did not want.

"You realize, of course," said the agent, "that Holyhead has no restaurant or sleeping accommodations at the station?"

"Why would I need those accommodations?" answered Rollie. "I plan to take the train to London before I stop."

"The boat arrives at 11:00 P.M.," said the agent, "and the train does not leave Holyhead until 7:00 A.M. If you insist on traveling second class, then you must wait in the train station from 11:00 P.M. until morning. With first class, however, they will allow you to remain on the boat until morning. In addition, breakfast is included with the cabin fare."

"Oh, that makes a big difference," Rollie said. "I appreciate your insistence upon first class!" Rollie shook his head and smiled. An Irishman takes such a long time to make his point, and he thought of the turf by the side of the road, the unguarded sheep, the bus driver, and all the other incidents that had demonstrated the Irishman's trust and faith in his fellowman. It's the foreigner who demands all of these explanations and clarifications; *if one had as much faith in the Irish as they do in us, it would be much simpler,* he thought. Perhaps the attraction of Ireland was as much in the beauty of its people as in the beauty of its land. And Rollie left the agency with the feeling that he had been treated with dignity and care, as a true gentleman—and he was feeling very pleased.

Rollie was not at all hungry, so as he left the agency he decided to walk to Grafton Street and look into a few of the shops. He had not yet purchased anything at all to take home as gifts, and he had only today and Thursday to do his shopping. He wanted to buy something for Barbara, perhaps a sweater or wool skirt, although he thought he would do much better selecting a sweater—he knew that size, and one could not get the "wrong" kind. He also wanted to get a few things for the children, and as yet he had no idea what; looking through the stores should help. It was quite by accident that he met Anna, just outside a men's shop, half-way between Trinity College and Saint Stephen's Green.

"Rollie, is that you?" Anna called, very surprised to see him.

"Anna!" Rollie said, and he had forgotten about the promised call. "What a surprise. How are you?"

"I'm delighted to see you. Did you just get in?" she asked.

"Yesterday afternoon," Rollie answered and suddenly remembered his promise to call Anna when he arrived in Dublin. "I'm sorry I didn't call then, but it slipped my mind. I hope I didn't upset anything," and on seeing Anna again, Rollie was embarrassed for not having called.

"Have you time for coffee?" Anna asked, and they both crossed the street to McDonald's. "Well," Anna began, once they had coffee and were seated near the front window. "We've planned a send-off this evening, so you've got to prepare for a good get-together," and Anna showed her excitement. "Now it won't be so grand as James would put on, but we'll do well," and she guessed that Rollie would know what she meant.

"You mean we won't try to drink all the Paddy in the house," Rollie confirmed her assumption.

"You guessed it. Everyone has work on Thursday morning, so we can't keep up with James during the week. And you want to leave Ireland with a clear head, don't you?" Anna smiled and squeezed Rollie's hand. "Have you made arrangements yet for your boat passage?"

"I just came from the agency," Rollie answered, "First class to Holyhead. The boat leaves at 8:00 P.M. from Dun Laoghaire, but I get the train at 7:30 at Connolly Station."

"That will give you plenty of time for dinner and a long sleep," Anna said. She looked at Rollie to see if he was really interested in tonight's little party. "You do want to come tonight, don't you?" she asked.

"Certainly. I wouldn't miss it." Rollie did not ask who would be there; nor did he ask the time. He just sat there, not knowing what he should do.

"I've called Myra, so she and Jack will be there. James is on holiday with Pat, so we'll have to get along without them. Do you still have your rental?" Anna asked.

"No, I don't," said Rollie, "but the bus will get me into town."

"Where are you staying?"

"At the Green Isle, just out on Naas Road." Rollie gestured, as though one could see from the restaurant all the way to Naas Road.

"Well, I'll pick you up," Anna said. "It's just a short distance from my place. You won't have to take any bus."

"That's no bother," said Rollie.

"No. I'll be there at six-thirty. Wear a white carnation in your lapel so that I'll recognize you!" Anna laughed and squeezed his hand again. Rollie laughed, too, and then they both were silent for a minute. It seemed they were thinking about the past week and the fact that tomorrow would be the end. Rollie pictured a Graham Greene character in his mind and wondered whether or not the end of this relationship could truly be termed "the end of the affair," and he looked intently at Anna, who by this time was looking, head bent, at their joined hands on the little table that separated them.

CHAPTER FOURTEEN

"And would you have forgotten to call me, as well?" Myra said, half seriously.

"I could not have forgotten such a wonderful hostess. After all, who was it who introduced me to all the wonderful people I have met this time in Dublin? That would have been barbaric of me." Rollie toasted Myra as he finished his reply.

"Ah, you say that," Myra said, "but I don't know that I believe you." Myra said a few more things about the '74 trip and the fact that Rollie had forgotten to call then.

"Well, it's true that there are so many wonderful things happening in this country, it takes one's mind off a lot of more important things. But really, Myra, I wouldn't have forgotten to call, not this time." The dinner party had started promptly at seven o'clock, and by this time, everyone had had about two drinks and was very talkative. Even Jack had struck up a conversation with Rollie, almost as though he saw an obligation to answer an earlier question that Anna had asked about Rollie. Jack found Rollie interesting and willing to talk about things that interested Jack.

"Have you seen any football games this time?" Jack asked, wondering if Rollie had attended the championship at Galway.

"I drove the car to an amateur game at a park just north of Galway one day, but that was all."

"Those games can be interesting," Jack said. "They don't care too much about roughness, and there are a lot fights, especially among the fans. We get a lot of those teams visiting Dublin; they like to get a fling at our local players from the east. They think we city folk are sissies."

"Do you ever get to go fishing?" Rollie asked, hoping that

Jack wouldn't mind a change in the topic. Rollie wanted to discover whether or not his choice of the Shannon at Athlone had been a good one.

"Not often, but once a year or so I get the chance to do a little on the ocean. A friend of mine owns a boat on the coast, and we spend a couple of days fishing and drinking. I never catch much, but we have a good time."

"I'd like to do that sometime," said Rollie. "I've got a friend in America who spends two or three months a year in Florida, on the Keys, and he does that kind of thing every day. He never tires ot it. If it weren't for the cost, I think I'd do it—at least once."

"It is expensive, especially the boat," answered Jack. "Even when you own it, the insurance, guide, and fuel are costly."

"The seven pounds I spent on the Shannon expedition," said Rollie (he liked to say expedition, since it was the first time he had spent an entire day on a boat) "seems such a little amount. At that time, I thought it was far too expensive, especially for what I was provided." Rollie continued to tell Jack about that day and his catch, and the description of the supper on the bank opened another conversation facet.

"Did you get any trout?" asked Jack.

"I hit a pickerel almost as soon as I dropped the line into the water," said Rollie, "and that got me so excited that I almost lost it. Then I discovered I had no net, no stringer, and no brains!" and Rollie laughed when he recalled the ludicrousness of that day. "If it hadn't been for the bread, wine, and cheese at the end of the day, the whole affair would have been a bust."

"Eating like that is great, isn't it?" Jack said as he smacked his lips. "It's a picnic without the salads and frills, just the way I like it."

"As a matter of fact," said Rollie, "it was pretty good. I think I sat in the rain for a while and didn't even notice.

It was now about eight o'clock, and Anna called everyone for dinner. She had arranged the table so that Myra and Jack sat on one side and she and Rollie on the other. Actually, Rollie sat opposite Jack and Anna sat opposite Myra, which facilitated conversation during dinner.

"Well, Rollie, what do you think of Ireland this time?" questioned Myra, breaking up the conversation Rollie and Jack had been pursuing. Myra always liked to get everyone involved in the table conversation.

"I have never had a more wonderful time," said Rollie. "Even the weather behaved well once I left Athlone."

"It's too bad you must leave," said Anna, now expressing more personal concern than she had when she and Rollie had parted the first time.

"I can't afford it. I don't see how you people can afford the prices here." Rollie was referring to the fact that the locals apparently paid the same prices for things as the visitors. "Why, potatoes are twice what we pay in America. And look how much you depend on them."

"I think most Europeans are resigned to the fact that about 40 percent of a salary is used to feed a family. We just don't think about it often, particularly when we don't have a family to support. Notice, we are all single," and Anna pointed to the others around the table.

"Maybe that's the reason you and Myra have such great figures; you don't eat much—or often," and Myra waved her hand at him in that gesture of mock disgust.

"How long will you stay in London?" Jack asked.

"Only one day. The boat gets to Holyhead Thursday night, but I'll stay on the boat until morning. Friday night in London will do it."

"You'll love the boat ride," said Myra. "When I went on holidays last year, James and I took the boat and had a fine time. It's just like a nightclub."

"Is it open after the boat docks?" Rollie asked, thinking it might be nice to spend an hour or so before retiring.

"Goodness, yes. Nobody wants to bed down that early!" Myra raised her water glass to indicate a drinker wanting more liquor. "And the walk around the deck is refreshing. It gives you a thirst."

"I am looking forward to the trip. But, really, I hate to leave here. It's been such a rewarding experience. I don't think I have ever enjoyed anything so much." And Rollie looked at each of the three around the table, as if to thank them personally for their part in this trip.

By 10:30 P.M., everyone appeared to be getting tired. Jack was the first to mention the time and the fact that he had an early-morning appointment. He asked Rollie if he could drop him at the Green Isle.

"Yes, thank you," said Rollie. "It is getting late."

"Jack, that's not necessary," said Anna. "I'll take Rollie back. After all, my working hours aren't as demanding as yours; I can take tomorrow as a holiday, if I choose."

"It's not a problem at all," said Jack. "This is a fairly early night for us, don't you think?" he said to Anna.

"Yes, Anna, there's no need for you to get the car out. Jack heads that way—somewhat," said Rollie, feeling that he should support Jack's suggestion, although by this time he would have liked a few minutes alone with Anna.

"Well, then," said Myra, "give us a kiss, and we'll hope to see you soon."

"Myra, you've been great to me. I'll get back again, and I hope I can bring the rest with me," Rollie said, referring to Barbara and the children. Rollie did kiss Myra and Anna goodbye. It was abrupt and awkward, but he didn't know how to avoid it. Anna and Myra stood waving as Rollie rode off with Jack toward the Green Isle.

That night, Rollie lay in bed thinking about the visit. He did have a much better time than he had anticipated, especially when he considered that he made no advance preparations. With the single exception of the sick day in Athlone, every day had given him a unique experience to remember. Of course, some of those experiences were not pleasant, but for the most part he could point to something during each day that pleased him. He started to think about having spent these days somewhere else and whether or not those experiences would have been just as good. Certainly it would have been warmer in America—had he remained at home—and accommodations would have been superior to those in Ireland. But would he have reveled as much in the countryside, in the beauty of nature? He thought how much for granted he took America, and he supposed that any native of a land takes his own home for granted. *We only visit other places because they are unfamiliar to us,* he thought, *and the beauty we observe might well be similar to that in our country if we had been observant.* But he reasoned that America was too modern and the unchanging people and places in Ireland were the essence of the beauty. And besides, the slow pace here gave one time to think and observe.

Tonight Rollie was not his usual tired self. He supposed that the sleeplessness was due mainly to the fact that he would be leaving on Thurdsay, and this knowledge produced some anxiety. He tossed for an hour or so and could not get to sleep. Finally, he got up and got dressed and walked down the hall in hopes that the bar would be open. There was no one except the bartender in the room, but Rollie walked in anyway.

"May I buy a drink?" he asked.

"Certainly. Good thing you caught me. I was just about to lock up," the bartender answered, but not at all irritated.

"We didn't have many tonight. It's hard to say when there will be a crowd. A good dinner, though."

"A lager, please," said Rollie. He was thirsty and the beer was appealing. "How late do you usually stay open?"

"It's indefinite during the week. Sometimes twelve midnight, other times a little later. Tonight was much lighter than usual." The bartender put a lager in front of Rollie.

"I wonder if there are many guests here tonight?" Rollie asked, just to engage in a little conversation.

"This morning they said it was full," said the bartender, "but you never know what it will be by the night. This time of year there are cancellations."

Rollie finished two beers and went back to his room. He still was not tired, but he assumed that the bartender would like to close, since Rollie had been his only customer. When he had closed the door to his room, Rollie walked to the far side of the room and turned on the television. He got only white on the screen, so he turned it off. At this point, he was sorry he did not have another Macken novel; it would have been a perfect time to begin reading. Rollie got undressed once again and climbed into bed. His luck was a little better this time, and with only minimal tossing, he fell asleep.

"Thank you, very much. I appreciate the call." Rollie hung up the phone and stretched. It was 8:00 A.M., and the operator had just made the wake-up call he had requested. Although he had not remembered the night before, when he had checked into the Green Isle, he had asked to be given the call on Thursday morning. Rollie always thought ahead about such things, and he did not want to miss an important reservation. He shaved and showered, dressed, and walked to the dining room for breakfast. Today it was overcast, but the weather didn't bother him this morning. He was thinking about the boat trip and didn't, even for a moment, realize that he must fill his day doing something downtown, since the boat did not sail until evening.

It was not until Rollie was drinking tea, toward the end of his meal, that he remembered about noon checkout and the two large, heavy bags he had to deal with. He frowned at the thought of carrying them on the bus and walking the several blocks from the quay to Connolly Station. The only alternative was to hire a taxi, which he could do, once he arrived at the quay. (He could have taken a taxi from the Green Isle, but the fare would have been more than he wished to pay.) *Well, the day will not be ruined simply because I must manage two pieces of luggage,* he thought, and he set them down outside his room while he closed the door and returned the key to the desk. The walk to the bus was short, but it convinced him that he certainly would hire a taxi when he got to town; he was not going to lug those bags farther than he must!

The ride to O'Connell Street went without incident; even the simple matter of chatting with the bus driver was missing. This morning, several passengers boarded at the same time as he, and one of the passengers was talking with the bus driver before Rollie had gotten on. There was room enough in the storage area for his bags, and after Rollie had secured them, he climbed to the upper level of the bus. Although he always had wished to ride there, he had never done so. *Today,* he thought, *is my last chance;* so he did it!

It took Rollie about fifteen minutes to get a taxi, and even when he managed to get one to stop for him, the driver was reluctant to take such a short fare. If Rollie had not suggested the ride was worth a pound, he might have been forced to walk and carry those heavy bags. Upon reflection, Rollie was not at all sorry about his offer. The driver was hesitant about not getting a tip, but he didn't put up a fuss. Rollie just said thank you and walked away. He climbed the steps to the platform, put his bags in the checking area, and started toward O'Connell Street to find something to do until seven o'clock. He had a little more than seven hours' wait to begin his next adventure.

The afternoon passed quickly for Rollie. On Wednesday, after he had talked with Anna, Rollie had bought a sweater for Barbara and a wool hat, scarf, and gloves for Aliceanne. This afternoon, he found several books for the boys, and, satisfied that he had the gifts he wanted, Rollie went to a movie. It was after 5:00 P.M. when Rollie left the theater, so he decided to walk toward the Abbey Theatre, remembering that he had seen an interesting restaurant in that general area. As he turned the corner on lower Abbey Street, Rollie spotted the restaurant. Although it now did not seem so attractive as he had remembered, he walked through the doors and sat at an empty table. There were very few customers sitting at the counter, and only one other table was occupied. Rollie waited for several minutes, but when no waitress appeared, he changed this seat and took a stool at the counter. He ordered an egg sandwich and a glass of milk. As had so often been the case, Rollie forgot how dry the egg salad sandwiches were made. This time the cook at least buttered the bread, although he did not use any mayonnaise. The light supper was rescued, though, when Rollie noticed some scones under the glass case on the counter. He left half the sandwich, but finished two scones and the milk, and as he left the restaurant he again felt that glow of happiness—a "scone glow" he termed it!

When Rollie had been in the theater, the overcast sky had

cleared so that now it was bright out and considerably warmer than it had been during most of the day. He almost began to whistle as he started back up O'Connell Street toward Connolly Station. He took his time, looking in the store windows as he passed, since there was still plenty of time before the train would leave for the dock. As he reached each corner along the way, he would stop for several minutes and watch people as they passed. It was odd, he thought, that when one pays little attention to crowds everyone seems like everyone else. Yet when one takes time to look carefully at each person, none walks the same, none looks the same, and none appears to be doing the same thing! *I should look more carefully at people,* he thought, and he continued on his way to the station.

The train moved quickly out of the station, and within ten minutes Rollie was boarding the steamer for Holyhead. He had a porter take his bags to the cabin, and after he had placed things to his liking, Rollie left his room and walked to the first-class deck. He walked to the bow of the boat and looked out over the harbor. He could see the opening to the sea, and as unaccustomed as he was to any body of water except a river or lake, he was shocked by the vastness of it all. It was the first time he could remember not being able to see the other side, and it frightened him somewhat. Within minutes, however, the boat began to move toward that opening, and the fright of that first glance turned to excitement. This was Rollie Welch's first ocean trip, and he knew he would love it.

CHAPTER FIFTEEN

The boat had not been at sea for more than twenty minutes when Rollie felt a hand touch his arm and give a little squeeze. He had remained almost fixed in the place at the bow of the boat, just staring at the sea as if in a trance. Not once had he glanced back at the coast he was leaving; he had become fascinated with the water and waves and the steady movement of the boat as it cut through the sea. He was startled by the touch because he had thought he was alone.

"Hello. Fancy meeting you here," came the ring of Anna's voice through the wind that was rushing past them.

"Anna!" Rollie said, completely surprised to see her. "I had no idea you would be on this boat."

"Well, you didn't give me much of a chance to talk with you Wednesday night, now did you?" Anna said, smiling and clutching his arm more firmly. Anna had decided to take holidays for the remainder of the week once she had talked with Rollie that Wednesday noon. She had intended to tell him about her plans after dinner, when, she thought, they would be alone. But as things turned out, the opportunity did not present itself, so she had decided to surprise Rollie on Thursday. It was a surprise.

"I'm surprised, really surprised! When were you able to get a ticket?" Rollie asked.

"I took care of everything on Wednesday, but I never got a chance to tell you. Remember, you left with Jack!" Anna pretended she was upset, then turned and smiled at him.

"Well, no matter. This will be a good trip. We'll have a fine time," Rollie said with moderate conviction. "Is Jack along?" Rollie suspected he was, and that would probably be best, but he hoped for a negative reply.

"Why? Do you miss him that much?" Anna teased.

"No. I just know that you two are always headed somewhere or other for a party!" And for the moment Rollie flashed back to his telephone call in Galway.

"As a matter of fact, Jack had an early-morning appointment that stretched into evening. He will be surprised when he discovers that I am not home tomorrow. We were to meet James and Pat—they're due back tomorrow—but I'm sure Jack will manage without me. He's done it before." Anna tossed her head in the breeze and then looked at Rollie. "Are you embarrassed that I'm here?" She sensed something in Rollie that had not shown itself a week ago.

"Not at all. I'm very happy you've come along." Rollie was beginning to feel more relaxed. "What do you say we go to the bar and have a Paddy?"

"Sounds fine to me. It's getting a bit chilly out here," and Anna followed Rollie down the steps and around the side to the door. Once inside the hallway, it was only a few feet to the bar. Rollie and Anna seated themselves at a booth next to a view of the sky, which by this time was beginning to display its stars. He ordered two Paddys.

"I didn't realize how cold it was outside," said Rollie as he rubbed his hands. "They're a little stiff." Of course his hands were not stiff, but this was his way of starting a converstaion, particularly when he had not imagined seeing Anna again. He was still a bit shocked.

"The drink is good," Anna said. "It always seems to taste better when you need to be warmed."

"It is good," said Rollie, still wondering what he could do with Anna for the next few hours. He had had his fling, so to speak, during that first week, and after the phone call in Galway, he had determined to put Anna out of his mind, to enjoy the remainder to the trip, and to return to the lake to tell the family of his experiences. Even when he got back to Dublin on Tuesday, he didn't call her, and he probably would not have seen her at all, had it not been for the accidental meeting on Wednesday afternoon. Now, with two days left, Anna had appeared most unexpectedly. In a way, Rollie was upset.

For the next hour, Anna and Rollie exchanged pleasantries, and for a long time Rollie kept himself at a distance. It was not until Anna started talking about Voltaire that Rollie showed some of the intellectual spirit Anna had remembered from that first meeting at the Connolly's.

"And did you think *Candide* a good example of what happens to power that becomes blind to the advances of science?" Anna asked, really trying to bait Rollie.

"If Voltaire had not been so incensed by a few clerics he knew, I think the book would have been done better. Did you notice how he let almost every situation be colored by either a direct or indirect attack on the church?"

"But the church was pretty corrupt then, wasn't it? And besides, Voltaire attacks the Jesuits more than anyone else, and you know that the pope did dissolve that order, at least for a time." Anna did have a good grasp of history.

"Yes, but you can't take Voltaire seriously. I am certain he wrote the piece to irritate people rather than to level a genuine attack on the church or the Jesuits." Rollie now was getting warmed to his argumentative best. "If he had really been serious, don't you suppose he could have done more with the 'best of all possible worlds' theme than simply to have Candide wrestle with it? Dosteovsky would have done a much better job." And Rollie knew that statement would make Anna take notice, for she did not like the Russian at all.

"Oh, now do you want to compare a spirited writer with a philosophical dullard like Dostoevsky!" Anna loved this.

"Dullard? How could any dullard write *Crime and Punishment, The Brothers Karamazov, The Idiot . . .* " And Anna interrupted.

"If it takes anyone that long to make a point, then the point certainly can't be worth making. Why, he repeats himself so much!" Anna was goading Rollie.

"If you follow *The Idiot* closely, you can see a parallel to the Christian savior. Now that's art at its best, not the writing of a dullard!" Rollie was very serious, but when he saw Anna smiling, he, too, smiled and ordered more drinks.

The two of them sat there talking until 11:00 P.M. and were unaware that the boat had docked until they noticed movement through the porthole. There were people walking around the platform, and Rollie assumed they were the second-class passengers who would not be allowed to remain overnight on the boat.

"I think I shall retire for the night," said Rollie. "I slept well last night, and tonight feels like another good one."

"Well, if you're leaving me, then I guess I shall do the same," and Anna started to move out of her seat.

"We might as well take these with us," said Rollie, and they both carried the newly poured drinks to the deck below. When they reached the cabin level, Rollie stopped and asked Anna if she'd care to stop at his cabin to finish her drink.

"I'd like that," she said. "No sense in going off to sleep while we still have a Paddy to finish."

"Well, come right into my mansion," Rollie said as he gave a gallant gesture and helped Anna over the ridge.

"Where is your cabin?" Rollie asked.

"Just two doors down," Anna answered. "It won't take a second to get there."

The two sat and sipped their drinks, talking a little about literature, but recounting the things that had happened over the time that Rollie had been visiting.

"I've had an excellent time," Rollie volunteered, "much better than I had thought I would have. When I left America so unexpectedly, I wasn't sure that I would meet anyone. Yet I've made some very good friends this trip."

"I'm very happy James and Myra invited us, too; otherwise I would never have gotten to know this American visitor!"

"There were times, out on the west coast, when I had wished you were with me. There were some beautiful sights; you'd have enjoyed it."

"I'm sure I would have," said Anna as she moved a bit closer to Rollie. There was one bunk in the cabin, but a bit larger than most. Anna and Rollie had sat down on the edge, and as the conversation drew on, they both gradually relaxed against the side of the cabin that ran along one side of the bunk. The Paddy was beginning to have its effect on Anna, although it would have been difficult for most to notice any change, since her natural manner was so carefree and warm. "Are you pleased that I've made this trip, Rollie?" Anna asked, now very serious.

"I am, very much so." And Rollie kissed her on the forehead, nearly spilling some of his drink on the bunk.

"I am, too," said Anna, and as she had during their first meeting, she leaned her head on his shoulder.

Rollie was relaxed and put his arm around Anna. He had had enough to drink so that he had lost many of the inhibitions that would normally show themselves at a time like this.

"Why don't you just rest like this," Rollie said, "and I'll wake you up when we must catch the train? But maybe you're not taking the train. Will you stay on the boat and return to Dublin?" Rollie had just assumed that she was on her way to London.

"I'm not returning until Sunday. It's London for me!" she said and struggled to get to her feet. Anna stood up and placed her glass on the stand beside the door.

"Rollie, my dear," she said, "we should get more comfortable if we're going to spend the night here." Anna slowly pulled her dress over her head and placed it next to her glass on the stand. Once she kicked off her shoes, she stood in front of Rollie naked, except for the little lace panties at which Rollie found himself staring. He was still leaning against the wall, startled at what was happening. He looked at Anna's lovely body, but the only thing that crossed his mind was the scene in *Catcher in the Rye* when Holden Caufield, in the room with the young prostitute, thought only of smoothing out her dress. Rollie wanted to jump up and smooth out the wrinkled dress on the stand and almost did, except by this time Anna had put her arms around his neck and kissed him gently on the forehead.

Rollie and Anna spent the night together, and although Rollie did enjoy the closeness of Anna, the warmth of her body next to his, it really was not the kind of thing he had wanted to happen. He had been happy talking with her, thinking about her, and wondering about the relationship between Anna and Jack. Rollie had not wanted to become part of a triangle, and, more than that, he wanted to return home and tell everyone about his wonderful trip. He did not want an affair with Anna to get to be part of the story. But he had allowed this thing to happen, and now he must deal with it. Rollie slept, but very uneasily. If he had had his wish, this whole day would have disappeared and he would have started the day over again.

On Friday morning, Rollie was awakened by a gentle knock on the cabin door. It was 6:15 A.M., and the porter had brought tea and bisquits. At first, Rollie was about to tell the porter to enter; then he remembered about Anna.

"Just a minute, please," said Rollie as he quickly got out of bed and into his pants, which had been lying on the stand. He opened the door.

"Your breakfast, sir," said the porter.

"Thank you very much. This shall taste good this morning," said Rollie.

"Should you desire a more substantial breakfast, sir, the dining room will be open until 7:00 A.M. Everyone must leave the boat at 7:15," said the porter.

"Thank you." Rollie closed the door and looked at Anna.

"Did you forget me?" she asked.

"I was so flustered," Rollie said, "I never gave a thought about your tea." Rollie placed the tray on the stand. "I'll go after him and ask for another portion." Rollie put on a shirt and slipped into his shoes—without socks—and pursued the porter. He found him at the cabin just past Anna's. "Pardon me," said Rollie, "but Miss Barton, Cabin Number Four, is in my cabin this morning. May I take her tea with me?" Rollie felt awkward.

"No bother, sir," said the porter. "I shall be there in a moment."

"Thank you." Rollie returned to his cabin, and, shortly afterward, the porter came with Anna's tea.

"There you are. I hope you have enjoyed the trip," said the porter, and Rollie wondered if he detected a wry smile.

"You're welcome. Yes, it has been very enjoyable," said Rollie, and he placed fifty pence in the porter's hand.

"Thank you very much, sir. Enjoy your ride to London." The porter closed the door and left Anna and Rollie alone.

"I didn't notice any effect from the water," said Rollie. "I thought perhaps the boat would sway somewhat."

"It was most comfortable," said Anna, throwing her arms about Rollie and kissing him good morning. "I feel wonderful this morning. What a fine time we had yesterday."

"Yes," said Rollie. "It was a good time, wasn't it." Rollie tried not to dampen Anna's spirits, and he forced a smile. Yet Rollie, thinking about the night past, was not at all happy with what had occurred. He looked at Anna, now sitting on the edge of the bunk, no more clothed than when she had first taken off her dress. Rollie was not used to such "reckless abandon," as he would term it. Even Barbara rarely bared herself to him quite so unashamedly as Anna. And this did not seem to fit the character of Anna that he had pictured in his mind, especially after his first meeting with her, as well as after the phone call and party. He knew she had gone away several times with Jack, but he had never imagined that Anna would act this way. Not only did the previous night puzzle him, but also this new freedom he saw emerging from within her.

By 6:45 A.M., both Anna and Rollie had finished eating. Anna had dressed and left Rollie to collect her things from her cabin. They would meet, in five minutes, just at the bottom of the steps that led to the exit platform. Rollie took little notice of anyone around him once he spotted Anna. She had changed her clothes and now was dressed as he had imagined she would. She wore a bright pink dress, loose-fitting, which seemed to fall in rhythm with her hair. *This,* he thought, *is the beautiful Anna I know,* and he shook his head at the contrast he drew between his night vision of her and this picture in the early morning light. Perhaps the trip to London would be as enjoyable as his earlier trips to Ireland's west coast. At seven-thirty, Anna and Rollie boarded the train and began the short journey to London.

The ride through the countryside was pleasant, and Rollie

relived, for a while, the experience of his trip from Dublin to Galway. Anna chattered away, commenting on the scenery, the remarkable likeness to Ireland, her first meeting with Rollie, the phone call from Galway, and all those things that now seemed to occupy her mind. Rollie listened, more politely than seriously, and could not seem to generate the same enthusiasm about it all as Anna. He was disappointed, and he could not understand this feeling. How could it be that just a few days before he had thought of little else than Anna, and now, with but one day remaining in his visit, he wanted to get her out of his mind? Rollie's thoughts shifted to Barbara and home.

Throughout the morning, Rollie heard little of what Anna said. He imagined Barbara and the house on the lake; he wondered what the children had decided to do with the remainder of their vacation. Did they miss him? Did Barbara miss him? He even began to question whether or not this visit to Ireland was important. Rollie began mentally reviewing his trip through the west and south of Ireland, bringing to mind the wonderful sights he had witnessed, trying as it were, to justify his decision to go abroad so soon after the '74 trip. At times he grew morose, not over any particular thing, but more through a feeling that he had betrayed his family. He could justify, from a teacher's point of view, the need for firsthand information that would make his teaching better and more authentic, but his feelings were unmoved by logic. At times he wanted to cry, and he had no explanation for this feeling. He could remember times in the States, when after a long and hard day of teaching, he would think of his daughter Aliceanne and a surge of emotion would bring tears of joy to his eyes; similarly the thought of Barbara standing on the deck of their house overlooking the lake and the silhouette of her body against the setting sun made him think he need never leave the lake to find all the beauty in the world. But here he was, on his way to London, in the company of a woman to whom he was attracted, but whom he knew so slightly, and with whom he must spend at least another twenty-four hours. This wonderful trip suddenly had lost all of the anticipated joy; it had now degenerated into an unpleasant task with which he must deal for the remainder of his stay.

"Would you like some tea?" Rollie asked. It was the first he had spoken to Anna in the past twenty minutes.

"I think I should enjoy some," said Anna, " and perhaps we might ask for some scones?"

"A good idea," said Rollie, and he left his seat to see what he could find. London was no more than two hours away, and Rollie welcomed this short respite; he needed to collect his thoughts and mentally make plans for the stay in London. Certainly he would not embarrass Anna by suggesting that they take separate rooms, yet he must somehow let her know that he did not intend to be unfaithful to his wife again. Oh, how Rollie wished this affair had never happened.

"Your tea, madame," said Rollie.

"Mademoiselle," Anna corrected him.

"Pardonnez-moi," replied Rollie in his decidedly American accent.

"Delicious scones," said Anna, "almost as good as home!"

"Yes," said Rollie, still wondering what he would do about London.

CHAPTER SIXTEEN

Regent Park was spectacle enough for a day's stay in London; Rollie and Anna enjoyed every minute of it. *Twelfth Night* was playing in the outdoor theater, and Rollie was happy as a child to have—finally—an opportunity to see a Shakespearean play performed in England and by an English cast. The afternoon was bright and warm, and the day seemed to inspire even the players. The intermission lunch of cold chicken and salad was delicious; it made one forget the dark restaurants and smoke-filled dining rooms. It was all so refreshing!

The day, however, could not blot out what had happened the night before, and Rollie kept drifting back to thoughts of Anna and the cabin. He wanted to believe it had just been a dream, but he knew it had been real. He did not understand how he could have allowed himself to be lured into the trap (he was unwilling to accept the fact that Anna had not forced him to do anything), and the more he thought of the matter, the more convinced he became of his own innocence. But he was determined to enjoy the present and not let his conscience interrupt a pleasant afternoon.

By five o'clock, the play had ended, so Rollie and Anna took the long walk back to the lodgings they had taken for the night. It was still very warm (for London), and there seemed to be no need to rush anywhere. They window-shopped as they worked their way through the busy section of the city, and that diversion was as pleasant as any other. Perhaps Anna had in mind to purchase something, but Rollie had even forgotten about the presents he had intended to get for Barbara and the children. As a matter of fact, by this time Rollie had been able to forget everything; for a few hours he was again a single man—without a care. The earlier problems he faced in anticipation of spending another night with Anna had disappeared; he was free to do as he pleased.

"Let's buy a trifling," Anna suggested as they stopped to look at some ornaments in a shop window.

"And what will we do with them?" asked Rollie.

"We'll start our own business here on Carnaby Street and make a fortune," and Anna tugged at his sleeve. "No need to go back to that dull, drab life of the civilized world and regular working hours with bosses," and she pirouetted around a lamp post.

"I had thought you were a little crazy, and now I'm certain of it. Shall I find you a crate around back to display your merchandise?" Rollie asked in a mock-serious tone.

"No. I'll just contract for the business, take orders, and send you out on deliveries," and she stopped to jump the six inches to the curb.

It was all very playful, just like a young couple, very much in love. No doubt those passersby who saw Rollie and Anna shook their heads at "the youth of today"—just as pleased with their show as they feigned disgust. And they were a young couple in love, at least for a few hours. Arm in arm they continued down the streets until at last they arrived at the Hutchins House, where they would spend the night.

At seven, they went out for a bite to eat; the previous hour had been spent at lovemaking. The light dinner added to the joy of the day, and Rollie was very pleased with himself. He had taken advantage of this opportunity, and it had turned out much better than he had hoped. *Why did I worry so much?* he thought. *No one really cares what I have done or intend to do. Life goes on regardless, so why not enjoy it?*

The night passed in yet another few hours of lovemaking. Those two bodies seemed made for each other, and Rollie and Anna were delighted with each other. Life certainly could be wonderful, and they were living all of this pleasure and beauty that was meant for them. Rollie could never remember having been so happy, so pleased with himself and with another. He had forgotten, completely, about that marvelous intellectual attraction Anna and he had had for each other. This night there was no mention of the great men and women of literature.

☆ ☆ ☆

It was Saturday and the thought of home crept back to mind. Rollie would be on the plane bound for home in less than five hours, and soon Ireland, England, and Anna would be part of the past. Although Anna talked steadily to him during breakfast and he answered, he had no idea what she was saying or the answers he offered. In a few hours, all this would be forgotten, he thought, and life would return to normal. Once again, he began to imagine that this was all a dream, that soon he would awaken and discover that nothing had changed.

Such thoughts were nonsense, and he knew it. Rollie had allowed himself to be compromised. He could not believe it was his fault, yet who else could he blame? Certainly it was no fault of Anna. If Rollie had not come to Ireland, Anna would have known nothing of him. Barbara had urged him not to take the trip, and he wanted to blame her. Yet he knew well that Barbara's urging did not force him to take this trip abroad. Were Myra and James the cause of all this? Yes, they had wanted him to enjoy himself, but they would never have encouraged nor supported this relationship. It was Rollie's fault, and he had that to take back home.

Rollie and Anna walked again to Regent Park and then to the National Gallery at Trafalgar Square. They witnessed a changing of the guard at the palace, but it was just the small and less auspicious one on the hour. They purchased a few things in the stores on Carnaby Street—Anna to supplement her wardrobe, Rollie to fill his gift list. At noon, they stopped for lunch and chatted about insignificant things that had occurred throughout the morning. It was nearing one-thirty and time for Rollie to leave for Heathrow, but they did not talk about that. They said nothing about the past two weeks; they said nothing about themselves and their feelings for one another. Later on, Rollie would wonder if that had been a sign of her disinterest in him; for the present, however, it had no meaning.

The final good-bye at customs took no more pains than their

first meeting at Myra's. Rollie kissed Anna gently, squeezed her hand, turned, and walked away. They made no plans for later on. Anna watched as Rollie climbed the stairs, and when he was out of sight, she left. It was a strange parting; more was left unsaid than is usual in these situations. But both Rollie and Anna had an understanding, although neither cared to talk about it. Perhaps it was the *"end of the affair,"* and who would be the wiser?

CHAPTER SEVENTEEN

Rollie suddenly realized that Barbara had just asked him a question, and he wondered how long she had been standing beside him on the porch.

"The lake does that to you, doesn't it?" she asked, realizing that Rollie had not heard her ask if he wanted another coffee.

"Oh, I guess I was miles away. What did you say?"

"Do you want a refill?" Barbara asked.

"Thanks. I don't know why I'm so contemplative this morning. Maybe it's the jet lag." Rollie had been home now for two days, but the excuse seemed plausible. He continued to stare at the water, and rather than think about the trip, he started to reflect on his life here at the lake and at school. Did he enjoy it? Was he as happy now as he had been a year ago? Why should one short trip to Ireland change his mind about all those things he had always treasured, Barbara, the family, his teaching, his running? For some strange reason, Rollie thought about running and how he and Jim would conjure up reasons why the wind invariably seemed to take its toll on the runner.

It was actually Jim who first noticed that no matter how calm the day might appear, one needed only to begin to run to discover just how strong that opposing wind was. Jim hypothesized that nature must really have suffered from all those runners and in retaliation, had determined to blow wind in the face of all runners. Jim further explained that the wind was in your face no matter which direction you chose and, if you retraced your steps on the second half of the run, the wind changed direction to accommodate you! The situation always persisted.

But Jim could be talked into an alternate theory. Rollie suggested that there were an unbelievable number of "runner haters" who did whatever they could to foil a run. Although he could not say for certain that it was true, Rollie believed that if Mother Nature were not to blame for the wind, then large truck owners were. He envisioned a truck with a large fan mounted on the flat bed, pointed at the runners and blowing in their faces. For some inexplicable reason, the truck driver knew the runners' routes and kept just far enough ahead of them so that the blowing was effective, but the truck unrecognized.

Jim countered with another theory, which involved a conspiracy among CBers. Jim explained that as soon as a driver spotted him running along the road, he radioed all his friends to get in their cars and head out toward the runners. Jim swore that the same cars, especially in rainy and snowy weather, would drive back and forth along the route trying to see how close they could get to the runners and how much dirt, snow, et cetera they could splash on them. "It must be that way," Jim said, "because I can be in the house for hours and never see a car go by, but just a quick change into my running gear and everyone wants to go for a drive!"

Rollie had been shot at on one of his outings. He had just made the four-mile turn and was heading back up the hill in front of old Kenyon's barn, about one and one-half miles from home, when it happened. It was a hot day, and Rollie was paying little attention to traffic as he tried to sprint up the last thirty or forty yards of the hill. He was about five yards off the side of the road, and as he glanced up he saw an old, badly rusted car coming toward him. He thought someone was leaning out of the window, and as the car drew nearer he could see what he thought was an arm pointed at him. As the car sped by, Rollie heard a loud crack, as if a rifle shot had been fired. He instinctively shielded his head and fell toward the field that ran along the side of the road. After several seconds, Rollie got to his feet and looked toward the car, which by this time had driven far enough away that he could no longer see the license plate. Aside from the scrape on his knee, Rollie was not hurt.

Two days passed before Rollie thought to mention this episode to anyone, but by that time it was too late to expect to discover the culprits. Barbara had asked him why he hadn't reported it to the police that morning, and Rollie couldn't explain. He guessed that the seriousness of it all never left an impact, especially in view of the many other things that drivers did to runners.

But none of this kind of thinking could erase Anna from his mind; nothing seemed to matter to him except her. Rollie got up from his chair and walked to the kitchen door. He went into the kitchen and placed his cup in the sink. He turned to look for a moment at Barbara, who was standing against the railing looking out at a passing boat. Then he quietly climbed the stairs to the bedroom, where he would once more pack his bags.

Rollie had decided to exchange this life for the one he had been living for the past two weeks. He refused to allow any thoughts of family and obligations to restrain him. He had convinced himself that, regardless of the consequences, he needed to be with Anna.

It would be two days later when Rollie would learn that Anna, in a most bizzare accident, had been killed en route to the boat at Holyhead.